The Book of
SINS

The Book of
SINS

by Chen Xiwo

Translated by
Nicky Harman

New Writing from Asia

Forty-six,
New writing from Asia,
Third Floor,
207 Regents Street,
London W1B 3HH.
UK.

The Man With The Knife was first published in World Without Borders
(Nov. 2011.)

English edition first published 2014.
Cover design by Mugdha Sadhwani.

Printed and bound in Great Britain
by CPI Books, Croydon, CR0 4YY.

This book has been selected to receive financial assistance from English
PEN's Writers in Translation programme, supported by Bloomberg and
Arts Council England. English PEN exists to promote literature and our
understanding of it, to uphold writers' freedoms around the world, to
campaign against the persecution and imprisonment of writers for stating
their views, and to promote the friendly co-operation of writers and the
free exchange of ideas.
www.englishpen.org

ISBN 978-988-16775-6-3

You have corrupted my imagination and inflamed my blood.
I am beginning to enjoy all this.

Leopold von Sacher-Masoch, Venus in Furs. Trans, anon.

Chen Xiwo once worked as a 'mamasan' in a Tokyo brothel. For many of his readers, The Book of Sins represents the pinnacle of his multiple award-winning writing career to date. Chen Xiwo was described by Asia Sentinel as 'one of China's most outspoken voices on freedom of expression for writers.'

Nicky Harman lives in the UK. She has worked as a literary translator for a dozen years and in 2011 was Translator-in-Residence at the London Free Word Centre. Authors she has translated include Dorothy Tse, Chan Koonchung, Yan Geling, Han Dong, Hong Ying and Xinran.

Contents

vii

This is a dark world. I can see that, even if you can't. When I tell you about it, you say, What you see isn't real. You're sick. Yes, I am a sick man. I am damned because I see a world you can't, or won't, see. Because I see the skull beneath the skin.

But you're no better off. You're like a frog that has been caught and thrown into the pot. The water warms up, you're a bit uncomfortable, but you can take it, and you're too lazy to move anyway. Then the water starts to boil, and now you want to jump out, but it's too late. You should have felt the pain much earlier. Then you could have jumped out of the pot and saved your skin.

Is being alive really such a big deal? I'm not sure. What's the point of living like a contented pig, without a scrap of dignity? In one sense, someone who dares not to live is more deserving of our respect. So I'll risk pissing you off, to show you life as it really is. Take a good look. I know you really want to, even though you find it offensive. I know you have a longing to be outraged, to suffer. We're all secret masochists. Take toothache: we know that if we touch a rotten tooth it will hurt more, but we still can't help probing it with our tongue, just to make sure. We need to be sure, even if it makes the pain worse. In fact, when the pain reaches a peak, it seems to lessen.

There is light even in the darkest of places. I insist that I am an idealist. The fact that I am prepared to offend my readers whatever the consequences to me, proves that. Of course, I can't compel you to share my idealism. I can only place this book in front of you, each chapter deeper and more terrifying than the last. Before you enter each one, I will ask you: Are you sure about this? You can shut the book now. If you still choose to read on, don't blame me.

Are you sure about this?
You can shut the book now.
Do you choose to read on?

Pain

1

Does it hurt? Have you got a headache? The kind that makes life not worth living. The kind that hits you when you wake up in the morning, even though there was nothing wrong when you went to sleep – no cold, no bad dreams, nothing. You just fell asleep, and when you woke up, there it was. Now your whole day is wrecked. All you can do is blunder through until it's time to go to bed again.

Then again, a toothache's much worse. Worse than anything. A toothache grabs hold of you and forces you to do something about it.

I've always had toothaches. I blame my mum. All our suffering is genetic, unless you get smashed up by a car. When I was a kid, my mum had a lot of faith in preventative education, but then she was a primary school teacher. She was always really worried about my teeth. She taught me to clean my teeth properly when I was three. 'You don't want to get teeth like your mum's,' she'd say. She went on and on about the terrible state of her own teeth, like an old woman, but seemed full of confidence about her daughter's dental health.

The trouble was, I could never hold the toothbrush steady, I just jabbed it all over the place. 'From top to bottom – at a 45-degree angle,' she'd sigh. 'Left side, right side, slowly, slowly, brush, brush … slow down, slow down. Remember: patience and perseverance.'

When we all had to do military drills, I stood on the school parade ground and kept thinking back to the training I'd had cleaning my teeth. My teeth earned me a lot of beatings, though they can't have been that bad – the pain has faded now. I never dared defy my mother. If I ever said 'no', she'd jab her long, straight forefinger at me and make me stand with my face to the wall for hours. I just knew I had to avoid toothache, whatever it took.

I was never allowed to eat anything sweet, even candied olives. I remember leaving school on Children's Day with armfuls of sweets – even the wrappers looked good enough to eat. But as soon as I got home, my mother grabbed them and took them away.

'People can do without sweet things, but they can't do without teeth,' my mother said. 'And once your teeth rot, you've had it.'

There was never any sweetness in my childhood. When I was a child, it was never: 'The big bad wolf will get you!' It was always: 'Your teeth will rot!' But they rotted anyway.

It started before I was five years old. I can see it clearly now. We were eating dinner – belly pork – when a sharp pain jabbed into my left molar. Cold sweat trickled down my spine, my mouth gaped. It wasn't the pain so much, it was more the terrifying prospect it opened up. My mother was staring at me in horror, so I shut my mouth and carried on chewing as if nothing had happened. But my mother wasn't so easily fooled.

'Open your mouth!' she commanded. I kept on munching.

'Open!' she shouted again, threatening me with her chopsticks. But before I could move a muscle, she threw them down in despair. 'I've told you a thousand times to brush your teeth properly. Properly! But you never listen.'

God knows I tried. I mean, I was worried about my teeth too.

The toothaches which followed were so awful I wanted to die. It was all my mother's fault, that was obvious, I'd inherited her teeth. The pain was unbearable.

As I lay in the dentist's chair for the first time I couldn't see his face behind the mask, all I could see were his eyes swivelling back and forth. I had no idea what he was going to do. I was full of imagined terrors. The instruments clattered in the metal dish as I gripped the arms of the chair.

The drill turned then stopped – a fierce warning – then approached my mouth.

I opened wide, not out of fear, but to please my mother, to ask for her forgiveness. The drill turned in my mouth. It didn't hurt, it just whined and tickled – it was almost pleasant.

It started to hurt, but only a bit. I could bear the pain. When it hurt more, I dug my fingernails into my palms and put up with it. I stuck my legs out, like a boiled frog, taking it, taking it, until I passed out.

I'll never forget that nightmare as long as I live. I gradually lost my teeth one after another. They were drilled, filled, and pulled again and again, with every conceivable kind of dental tool, but it was always the same.

'All I can do is kill the nerve,' said the dentist, rapping on a sore tooth.

'That way it won't hurt,' said my father. 'Pain comes through the nerve.'

My father was a medical man too, a doctor. He thought that the science lesson would calm me down, but it only made me worry all the more. Our bodies are covered with a dense mesh of nerves, he said, with blood flowing through countless veins and arteries. As the blood brushed the artery walls, a nerve might crackle into life, like an electric spark. The thought terrified me.

My head was full of weird ideas like this. When my face got red in PE I'd say 'It's the blood rushing to my head.' If someone had a cold, I would explain how the white blood cells were locked in battle at that moment with the invading germs. It didn't make me any more popular, in fact I think it made my classmates sick. I wasn't even popular with the teacher.

She was never very sympathetic when I said I was in pain.

'What are you talking about?' she asked.

'But it hurts!' I protested.

'You're such a little flower,' she said, and pointed to the class monitor. 'Why can't you be more like her?'

The class monitor was a tough one, even though she was a girl. She was very grown up, too. Once she fell into an uncovered drain on the way back from school – she just crawled out with a huge bump on her head and a broken hand. The highways department tried to make out it was all her own fault, but she stood up in front of the class, her head held high and her bump throbbing, and told us all how she conquered the pain. At the end she raised her arm in salute but came up short – the sling got in the way. Still she didn't flinch. How come it didn't hurt? I flinched, just

4

looking at her.

I've been through agony. Headache, toothache, backache, bruises, sprains, torn muscles – they've hounded me with intense, raw pain all my life. I've thought about ending it all, but that would hurt even more, wouldn't it? On the other hand, once you're dead there's no more pain, and that's some sort of liberation. I used to rack my brains for a way to die that didn't hurt. Jumping into a river? Hanging myself? Cutting my veins? Maybe overdosing on sleeping pills – after all, it couldn't hurt once you were asleep. I started sneaking into the pharmacy at my father's hospital, messing about and chatting up the technicians while I figured out which brown bottle held the sleeping pills. I'd steal a few when they weren't looking. Just a few – I didn't want to get caught.

Planning ahead came easily to me. I didn't dare keep them at home, in case my parents looked in my room, so I tucked them in the lining of my pencil case and carried them around in my school bag. Setting out for school every morning was like saying goodbye for the last time. I'd slip away with a long, sad look at all the familiar things I was leaving behind.

Then there was something on the news about some woman who'd killed herself with an overdose. Her face was bright purple, as if she'd been strangled.

'But she just took too many sleeping pills,' I blurted out. 'How can that hurt?'

'What makes you think an overdose isn't painful?' my father asked.

My heart sank like a stone. It seemed impossible to die without pain.

'What a crazy kid!' said my mother. 'You're too young to think about dying.'

2

My periods started when I was thirteen – and so did the period pains. Once in biology it hurt so much I rolled off my chair and under the desk. The teacher rushed me straight off to the sickroom.

'Just your time of the month,' said the nurse.

But I was in such pain that I couldn't help rolling around on the bed. The lesson finished and my classmates clattered down the stairs, making the whole building shake. They crowded round the sickroom door – I was so ashamed. There was nothing I could do. Some of the boys even started calling me names. Then the biology teacher came and chased them away.

'What do you think you're doing? What's all the fuss about? It's a normal thing that happens with girls' bodies!' All the boys ran off shouting.

It was so embarrassing. The boys gave me weird looks, like I was that plastic model of the human body in the lab and they were taking me apart to read my secrets. And the girls ignored me, because somehow, through me, they'd become specimens too and I'd revealed their secrets. When we had to line up separately, boys and girls, the girls bunched up together and left me on my own. It was as if I was a different sex, as if they didn't have periods, as if the ads for sanitary towels on the TV weren't aimed at them. They were ever so careful to stuff their sanitary towels firmly inside their knickers so they wouldn't show. They talked and laughed as if there was nothing going on. If the PE teacher asked them to run the 1,500 metres, they just ran. But I couldn't. I wanted to act like normal, when I had a period, but I couldn't keep running. I made a fool of myself again: I tripped and fell over. The school called my parents and I was sent off to my father's hospital.

An old man was bent over at reception, gripping on to the bars of the window and vomiting out his guts. Where were his family? My dad took me straight in – no need to wait in the queue, or register at reception – and they started all the checks: temperature, blood pressure and so on. So much for special treatment. Every patient has to be checked over, even top Party officials, special treatment or no.

The doctor ordered me to lie down and take off my trousers. I was really embarrassed, even though it was a woman. Suddenly I felt a strange, tearing pain. All my nerves went into spasm. For the first time I really noticed that part of my body. It hurt. But that hand was pitiless, the way it pushed itself inside. Then she stood up and washed her hands.

'There's nothing the matter.'

Nothing the matter? I was obviously still in pain. She sat down at her desk.

'I'll write you a script for the herbalist.'

Herbs? That wasn't going to work in a hurry. You had to pick them up from the pharmacy, take them home, soak them, cook them, then steep them again like tea ... I'd seen my mother do it a thousand times. But this pain was so severe I couldn't bear it for another second!

'I don't want herbs! I want western medicine!' I screeched.

7

The doctor was surprised. Then she looked at my dad and smiled. 'She knows a lot about medicine for such a young girl.'

'Herbal medicine has fewer side effects,' my Dad put in, smiling back.

'I don't care about side effects! I want western medicine!'

She smiled again and stroked the back of my head. 'There's nothing the matter.' She'd said it again. What was she on about? There was nothing wrong with her, obviously, she wasn't in pain. I just wanted to curl up under the bed.

'I don't want herbal medicine!' I wailed.

Eventually I got my prescription. But it didn't do any good. A month went by and it hit me again. I was rolling around on the floor in the middle of the night, all sticky. I was rolling around in blood.

My room was wrecked. The bed was messed up, the clothes were all over the floor and my sheets were tangled round the legs of the table. My mum panicked and begged Dad to go fetch his friend, the director of gynaecology. He went off and my mum started clearing up the room, yelling at me to get up. But I just couldn't, even when she tried to drag me to my feet.

'What's the point in lying on the floor,' she shouted. 'How's the floor going to make it any better?'

But the floor did make it better. I was at one with the blood, the mess and the dirt. I pressed my face against the tiles and gave them a kiss. She pulled at me and slapped me and my face burned and I started to sob. My mother opened the door and the director came in, bringing the cold night air with her. I stopped crying and looked at her feet. They were very bony, like a wise, old face. I crawled nearer. Lying in front of her, I started to hope she might save me.

She bent down to me, stethoscope at the ready, and listened to my chest. I longed for her to find a symptom, to tell me what was wrong.

Her face was as blank as her feet. She stood up slowly and put the stethoscope back into her pocket. She asked my father to show her what I was taking. Was it the wrong medicine? Maybe she'd start criticising the doctor who'd prescribed it and give her the sack. After all, she was the head of department. But she didn't do any of that.

'Just keep taking those,' she said.

It was as if the lights had gone out. Couldn't she see when someone was ill? What kind of a director was she? Was she just in the job for the perks?

'Once she's married, it'll get better.'

Dad stumbled out his thanks, took her to the sitting room and shut the door.

Get better once I'm married? Why? I had no idea. Surely marriage would bring even more pain? All that rubbing, that pressing … and what about giving birth? All that straining – your womb swollen, the skin stretched tight, the vagina torn as that thing forces its way through. There would be no salvation then. All you could do was repent. Repent getting married, repent growing the vile seed inside you. Why were all these women so over the moon about girls getting married, having babies, living like this? It seemed like a con to me. The director of gynaecology conned the sick, old crones conned the young, mothers conned their daughters, pregnant women conned themselves and as soon as the pain was over, they started thinking about another child. Couldn't they remember? Was there no end to suffering?

3

It wasn't the gynaecologist's fault. She really was a very good doctor. But if there was nothing a doctor like her could do for my pain, then what was the point of medicine?

I only made it into the world thanks to her. I was a breach baby. They asked my dad if they should save the mother or the baby. He said the mother, of course – it was what everybody said back then. But the operation was a success – in fact a pioneering success – and my long-suffering body survived. Maybe that's why I resented the gynaecologist.

My father also used to go around with a stethoscope and a white coat. He would stand very straight by the bed with his hands in his pockets, and as he watched the patients writhe and cry out in pain all he would do was push his specs back up the bridge of his nose. He was used to it.

He was a doctor. The bottom line for him was saving lives, even if the patient wound up a vegetable. That was all he knew how to do.

My father always stood up tall, until the day liver cancer felled him. Everyone said he'd got the wrong disease. He didn't smoke, or drink, or eat pickles or any fried food. He had none of those bad habits which are supposed to cause cancer. If you were superstitious, you'd say that it was because Yama the King of Hell hated him for snatching so many people from its jaws. But I reckon he got ill because he had seen so much suffering. A doctor can't live the good life, spouting the kind of pleasant bullshit people want to hear. May you live a long, long life. May you be prosperous. May you enjoy your rest. No, doctors have to face up to the relentless cruelty of human existence.

Without his white coat, my father lost all his dignity. Those coats look after doctors even better than the Party looks after its members. Other people get sick, catch diseases, die … but not doctors. As soon as he was diagnosed, my father was reduced to a mere mortal.

Frail and helpless, they wheeled him from surgery to radiotherapy, from radiotherapy to chemotherapy. He used to plead with his old colleagues like a child as they prepared him for treatment: 'I don't want it! I don't want it!' Stage four cancer is horrifically painful.

No one could save him. All we could do was watch and weep as he shrivelled up. At the end he was nothing but skin and bones. He had been a big man, 1.8 metres and 73 kilos, full of energy for all his forty years. Now something unimaginably powerful was crushing that vitality out of him.

'Dad,' I asked. 'Does it hurt?'

'Yes,' he said, and then more loudly, 'life is just a big trap, and I fell right into it!'

My father knew he wouldn't get better right from the start. He knew far more about it than the rest of us. He was a doctor. We made pathetic attempts to deceive him. Sometimes we told him he looked better, plumper in the face. Other times, we said his tumour had reduced in size, or that before the year was out there would be a new, groundbreaking anti-cancer drug. He just smiled. His smile was all that was left of him, but sometimes it allowed us to believe, naïvely,

11

that there was hope.

One of the doctors looking after my dad had worked under him as a junior doctor, and had become his assistant. In those days, he was my father's shadow – they would go everywhere together. Three days before my dad died, he stopped his assistant while he was doing the rounds.

'Give me some pethidine,' he said.

The doctor flinched as though he had been knifed in the ribs. Pethidine is an opiate – everyone thought it was as bad as heroin. He opened his mouth to speak, but my father stopped him with a look. The assistant left the room without a word.

My father was very dignified while he was dying. He just lay there quietly until he sank into a coma. Once he called my name, his voice filled with an extraordinary calm. I was amazed to see how he accepted death.

Another time his colleagues were conferring in whispers by the window, the sunlight pouring in and giving them a sort of fantastical halo. And then he said it again: 'Pethidine.' I'll never forget the look of panic on their faces.

4

My father's assistant was always there when me and my mum visited the hospital. If he was sitting down, he would stand up straight away, arms by his sides. If my dad wasn't with him, he would say politely 'Ah, the Director is…'

After my dad died, I bumped into him at the hospital.

He stammered out 'Ah, the Director is...' and blushed scarlet.

I smiled and finished it off for him '...in the grave.' He smiled back and said he was sorry.

I was always bumping into him at the hospital, accidentally on purpose, of course. I liked the way he panicked whenever he saw me, like a rabbit in the headlights. I used to go straight to his consulting room and lean against the examination couch, watching him. He'd carry on, but he knew I was there. His colleagues would come in and give me a knowing smile, but I didn't care if they thought something was going on between us. I liked it. He was always embarrassed. After the patient left he'd make a clumsy show of surprise, as if he'd only just noticed me. 'Oh! Were you looking for me? Is something up?' He wouldn't even look at me. He'd just stare at the wall, as if he was talking to the poster hanging there. It read: 'The Party is our mother and our father. Patients are our family.'

'You mean I can only come looking for you if something's up?' I asked.

Now he was confused. I liked seeing him in a fix. He looked like a thief. All men are really thieves – I was just persuading him to follow his instincts.

Of course I knew what would happen if I carried on like this. Pain. That was the price I'd have to pay. I'd never been in love, was never going to be. But would I be able to avoid the pain of making love? That gynaecologist who'd burrowed so brutally into me said that things would be better when I was married. But I could remember the pain, the way my vagina went into spasms. I still had bad dreams about a drill tearing into those walls and bloody red pulp gushing out.

For women it is pain and more pain. Pain is a woman's fate.

When Chairman Mao asked his ministers how to get a cat to eat a chilli, Liu Shaoqi said to starve it for two weeks. Zhou Enlai, said to hide the chilli inside a piece of fish. But Mao shook his head.

'Stick the chilli up the cat's arse,' he said. 'The cat licks where it hurts, so it eats the chilli. The more it hurts, the more it licks.'

The more it hurts, the more it licks ...

My dad's assistant told me it takes time for feelings to grow, that he didn't believe in love at first sight. He was like a key fitting tooth by tooth into a lock, with his fine words. He was pure reason, but I was a piece of trash. I loathe reason. Reason is the sort of rubbish you can indulge in when life is sweet, like love and honour. I totally reject it. The way he said the word 'marriage' made it sound so right and proper, but he couldn't see how it was tearing me apart.

I hated it when he took me out shopping, or to the cinema. I detested sitting in tea houses, sipping all sorts of brews. I couldn't stand going to western restaurants, hacking at a slab of steak with a fork in my left hand and a knife in my right. And he would just sit there, cold and uncaring, bragging about his qualifications. I told him he was just like Zhang Yimou. He wasn't happy about that at all.

'What do you mean?' he protested. 'He's just a director. He's only famous because his films get good reviews. I've got exams.'

He could never bear the cheating that went on in examinations. He wanted so much to believe in them, to believe he had got into medical school purely through his own talent. But it's pathetic to take an exam, whether you cheat or not. People with real political clout never need to sit them, they make other people study hard and take the tests, they control the system.

Once he brought all his certificates along in a briefcase.

'This is my capital,' he said, as he showed them to me, one by one. 'All my capital!'

I pictured him laying them out every night on the bed in his room like a winning hand of cards, then flinging himself down beside them in an ecstasy of delight. As for me, I was like a whore touting her pussy, or rather a girl trading her virginity and finding there was no one who was willing to invest.

I shoved his precious certificates away. What good were they for a headache or a sore foot? He quickly put them back in order.

'This is science,' he said, like a primary school kid putting on his red scarf for the first time. He knew all about science, he had all sorts of technology at his fingertips. But sometimes it seemed he didn't really believe in it.

'If everything goes well, I'll get promoted soon – the first in my year to get a proper job.'

He was always very careful with his prescriptions, even lowering the dosage sometimes, thinking that the slightest mistake could ruin his career. He used to tell me that his family was different to mine.

'My grandfather was a peasant, my father was a factory worker and now I'm an educated man,' he said. 'I love my job, but it wasn't easy to get here.'

Sometimes I prayed he would screw up and prescribe poison. He'd be destroyed – it wouldn't do him any good loving his job then. But every time he wrote out a script,

Chen Xiwo

he'd tilt up the pad and check it over. He even shredded his old pads. I could never get hold of one.

My mum knew I was up to something, even though I never breathed a word. She must have figured my pain would lead me to do something stupid. After my dad died, our home crumbled, leaving my mother pitiably, ridiculously, alone, a pillar left standing in the ruins of the Summer Palace. She worried about me more and more. Every time I cried out 'It hurts!' she'd snap back 'Why are you wailing like that?' My illness scared her. It was as if I was a ghost howling at her. Howling at the whole world.

The doctors all knew about the famous clinician's daughter who had this terrible illness. Did doctors pass down disease to their children, they wondered. But no one lifted a finger to help me.

Mum would tell me how her generation had lived – putting things to rights after the Cultural Revolution, the Reform and Opening Up period, respecting education, developing the economy, the fight against corruption, the progress towards a glorious future.

'Your generation is so lucky, what more do you want? You just don't know how lucky you are … '

But the word 'glorious' was like hitting a gleaming pane of reinforced glass – I was in more pain than ever.

'What more do I want? I want to be happy!' I shouted. 'You think I'm really happy? I'm in pain, I've been in pain ever since I was born! You shouldn't have had me if you couldn't give me happiness. Why shouldn't I go and look for happiness myself?'

'Of course there's still a dark side to society,' she admitted. It was something she would never have said before. 'There are

16

people out there who who pretend they know just what you're going through, but actually they're just trying to get you on to their side. The dark side of society,' she continued, whispering now, 'comes from the speed at which society is developing, a speed which has produced psychological disorders in some people. It's a problem we will have to face …'

So it was just psychological? Hadn't she seen me sick for the last 20 years? She was behaving like some big doctor, more doctorly than any doctor, brandishing her miracle cure. No. It wasn't true. I didn't have a psychological disorder. I was just in pain. It had nothing to do with the dark side of society. I was just in pain. Pain. Pure pain!

I hated the way no one would really treat my illness. I hated the strange way my mother wanted to deal with it instead. I hated her logic. She was so complacent.

'So how come all you did was cry when dad was sick?' I asked. 'Why did you let him die in so much pain?'

'You think you're the only one in pain?' my mother howled back. 'I hurt all over too! I've had all sorts of gynaecological problems. Eroded cervix, inflamed pelvis, obstructed fallopian tubes. None of it's ever cleared up. I don't go around shouting about that, do I? No one should ever expect to be completely well!'

I looked at her in astonishment. She was drowning in her own despair. I burst into floods of tears, crying like a helpless baby.

'A girl shouldn't let people think she's too easy!' my mother yelled.

'Easy?' So she was calling me a whore. I ran out of the house.

It was a moonless night. As I walked down the street a

17

car alarm went off and the neighbours poked their heads out between the bars of their security grilles – frightened birds shut away in their luxurious cages. Every possession was guarded by alarms, defended by metal bars with reinforced, galvanised, stainless steel tubing, protected by lock after lock as if otherwise it would just fly away. A locksmith society. A society where prescription medicines had given way to quack remedies. A society where all our troubles would be solved by city-building, share-trading, property-holding, piano-playing, English classes, Peking opera classes, the internet economy and the virtual world. But it had nothing to do with me. I was a whore.

I went to the hospital accommodation block and knocked at his door. The assistant opened the door and I collapsed at his feet. He picked me up and panicked and pulled me inside.

'I'm in pain!' I cried.

'Where?'

'Everywhere!'

Of course, I wasn't in any pain at all. I was just making it up.

Now I was pretending, I could see pain was nothing to fear. I was writing pain on to my body as if I was writing it on to a piece of paper. I struggled and yelled so skilfully that it was more convincing than the real thing.

'Please! Stop screaming!' he begged. 'Someone'll hear!'

He was starting to sweat. I carried on screaming.

'I'm begging you! Stop screaming! I'll go and get you some medicine.'

'Medicine! It doesn't do any good! I've had this all my life!'

'OK … then I'll tell your mother.'

'Don't you dare tell my mum. I'll die right here in your

room!'

He went pale.

'So what do we do?'

'Give me some pethidine!'

It was as if my father was talking. His stern, commanding tones rang out, pronouncing the name of that blessed, addictive drug that allowed people to live and die with dignity. The assistant grew paler still.

'But that's a controlled drug!'

'Give me some pethidine!'

The three syllables landed like blows from a whip.

'Stop saying that!' He didn't care if anyone thought he was up to no good with a woman in his room, so long as they didn't hear us talking about pethidine.

'You don't realise how addictive it is …'

'Give me pethidine!' I insisted, like a vengeful spirit.

'Listen …'

'Pethidine!'

He fell silent.

He went across the room, opened the door and swung round.

'No more noise.'

5

At last there was no pain. For the first time ever. No pain. So this was happiness. His bed was very soft. His room was spacious, spanned with an A-frame of beams. A furled mosquito net hung down like a whip, twitching in the breeze. My body was strangely empty, waiting for something to fill it up. Was this love? I called his name, but he didn't answer. He just stood there, looking at me as if I shouldn't be so happy, as if it wasn't me any more, as if it was only me when I was sick and racked with pain. I had no right to be happy.

'To be honest, I wasn't really in love with you before,' I said.

I didn't care if he was shocked, if he was angry. He'd forgive me and take me in his arms. But he just sank down on to a chair. I felt so sorry for him. I stretched out my arms to embrace him, but he jerked away as if a terrifying hole had opened up before him. Was he so inhibited he couldn't take happiness when it was offered to him?

'It's true!' I said. 'Honestly. All I really wanted before was that … '

I pointed to the empty syringe on the bedside table. He shot out of the chair and rushed over to pick it up, jabbing his hand on the needle. I grabbed him and started to suck at the wound. I loved him. But again he jerked away, as if he had been electrocuted. I put my arms around him and held him tight.

'It's all my fault! Blame me, hit me if you want!'

He pushed me away and stood up

'I'm taking you home.'

'I'm not going!'

'OK,' he said. 'I'll go and sleep in the office.'

'No!' I screamed. I threw myself at him. He backed away, as if scared by the warmth of my body. My pain flooded back, a sharp pain like a cold wind blowing over a rotting tooth. My happiness had gone up in flames, disappearing like a smile on a photograph thrown on to a raging fire. Why couldn't he stay?

'Just give me a little bit more!' I begged him, grabbing at his arm.

He wrenched away from me, terrified, and leaped for the door, still clutching the empty syringe and dripping blood.

I grabbed it from him and he yelled 'What are you doing?'

I didn't know what I was doing. All I knew was that it hurt, just like when I was a child lying in the dentist's chair. I wanted it to stop. I wanted to kill myself. Or I wanted to make myself hurt all over, to be saturated in pain and happiness. Or I wanted to cut out my emotions, I wanted to kill them. I jabbed the syringe at my chest. He threw himself at me and snatched my weapon. I hung on to him like grim death.

'You're crazy!' he yelled. His body reeked of formaldehyde.

So the world thinks I'm crazy. The world is dead to me.

6

He turned himself in, saying he couldn't forgive himself for prescribing pethidine illegally. He got off scot-free. Pretty soon he was the mainstay of the unit, hailed as a model doctor. He probably did a deal with them.

When he took me to rehab he told me he no longer believed I was in love with him. They tested my blood and my urine – there was nothing wrong, but they wouldn't let me out all the same. Maybe they were just jealous I had felt the ecstasy of pethidine instead of the pain of ordinary life.

'Did it really feel that good?' they would ask, greed glinting in their eyes.

'Try it for yourselves.' I said.

'We can't do that,' they said, suddenly serious. 'We're here to make you better.'

They told me my family had come to see me. They led me down the corridor to the visitors' room, past the noticeboard full of press cuttings about the assistant's high principles, the banner with the glorious slogan: 'Say goodbye to drugs! Make a new life!'

He was standing with my mother – I hadn't expected that – his arm around her shoulder as if she was an old woman. She smiled as if she was being looked after by a dutiful son. But she was just putting on an act, trying to make me forget real happiness.

'We're waiting for you,' he said solemnly, as if it was something to do with him.

'Waiting for me to do what?'

'To come out!' Mum said.

'Come out and do what?'

'Just come out...' she smiled. 'Silly girl. We can begin a new life.'

I smiled too, and said with a touch of pride: 'But you don't understand pain.'

Are you sure about this?
You can shut the book now.
Do you choose to read on?

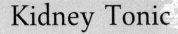

Kidney Tonic

1

Let me tell you this: I lead a pretty good life. We're always being told how much better off people are nowadays, but in my case it happens to be true – I've got plenty of cash. Ten years ago I took a few risks and I struck lucky. Then – because wealth and beauty go together – I married my beautiful wife. We live in a seventh floor flat in a smart residential district, with a lift, of course. From our balcony I enjoy a pleasant view over a landscaped garden – complete with a European-style arched gateway and fountain – where people from the neighbourhood stroll around or do tai-chi. The couple from the flat upstairs used to walk there every evening, the man whispering into the woman's ear, the woman smiling – they were about the same age as us. They'd take an evening stroll whatever the weather, their heads bent together under an umbrella or sunshade. Once they'd done a tour of the garden, they'd leave and come back across the main road.

There are some flash cars parked there, slotted bumper to bumper like a colourful jigsaw – the beige Honda Accord with the cuddly toys piled up in the rear window is ours.

The toys belong to our daughter. Yes, we have a daughter, and very pretty she is too. As the saying goes: marry a beautiful woman and you'll never have an ugly child. I tease my daughter all the time. I love pinching her until she goes red in the face and begs for mercy. 'What a doting daddy you are!' my wife says, poking me with her elbow. The pinching is just my way of showing how much I love her – she's too adorable for words. As soon as my wife and I start talking, she tries to talk over us. There's no way she's going to be left out of our grown-up conversation. She's a natural at butting in. When we go to bed at night, she pushes right in between us. As you can imagine, that means her mum and I never get up to anything. But why should that matter so much? We're a happy family, we have a lovely kid, we're quite satisfied as we are. Our daughter sleeps between us – my wife tucks in the quilt on her side and tells me to tuck in the other side.

We always used to feel very secure. We only shut the windows at night when we had the heating on, or the air conditioning. Of course that was mainly because we're seven floors up. So it was a shock to discover there was someone watching us from the building across the street. I noticed them while I was doing my exercises on the balcony. There was a flash from the window directly opposite – I shut my eyes out of instinct. I thought I must have imagined it, but as soon as I opened my eyes again there was another flash. A shadowy figure was watching at the window. I rushed back inside the flat.

I don't know why I was in such a panic – my wife and I had no secrets – but I rushed round shutting all the windows. All the details of our daily routine – everything we did, what my wife was wearing – started to prey on my mind. For example, my wife always went around in her nightie. Here in the south lots of people go out shopping in their pyjamas, but I was still uneasy. To my mind certain things are private, like the way you go to bed or what you wear while you're sleeping. No matter how proper my wife's nightie was, it was no one else's business. I had to hide it from prying eyes.

I started to think about our day-to-day life – were we doing anything wrong, anything which could be seen as inappropriate? Did we keep ourselves out of sight when we changed our clothes? Did my wife always shut the bathroom door before hitching up her skirt when she was going to the toilet? Was I still doing up the belt on my trousers when I came out? Life was full of difficulties. If I met someone when I was leaving the flat, I found myself turning away from them as if I had something to hide. That couple strolling in the garden were always smiling as I watched them from our balcony. Were they laughing at me? I couldn't shake the feeling that eyes were boring relentlessly into my back. I tried spying on the flat opposite, but the windows were always tight shut – it was as if they had never been opened. That made them even more sinister. I was sure there was someone standing behind them but I couldn't see the expression on his face. What was he thinking? Was he smiling? What at? I didn't know. Dammit, I didn't know! I only knew he was watching me. It was unbearable.

One day – just like that – I went across to the building opposite and took the lift to the seventh floor. The flat had no security grille, as if no one had ever lived there. I broke in through the bathroom window to find the place empty and deserted. It had grey walls and a concrete floor thick with dust. Mine were the only footprints. I looked across to our flat. I could see our silvery aluminium window frames, the blue panes of glass and the pale blue curtains. Our bedroom. A bed. Someone lying on the bed. A man. For a moment I thought I was looking at myself. How many times had I warned my wife to keep the curtains closed? The bedroom door was shut and I saw myself lying there covered with a big red counterpane, like an offering in a temple. But of course it wasn't me, it was another man, and it wasn't our flat – it was the flat above. His hand was doing something under the covers and his eyes were shut. His face became more animated, his eyes glittered and his hand started jerking. I could almost hear him pant and smell his breath. The breath of a male, just like me. I felt as if something was gripping my crotch, a hand, a man's hand, warm and moist. I was appalled...

I didn't tell my wife what I'd seen in the upstairs flat. I didn't tell anyone. I guess it's hard to talk about that kind of thing. It's OK to talk about assault, robbery, murder or even rape, but not wanking. We've all done it, after all, but what if people started talking about that? So I just kept quiet. But I couldn't forget what I'd seen.

He was always whispering sweet nothings into his wife's ear as they strolled in the garden. My wife always said they looked like a courting couple, but I just smiled and said nothing. All that whispering was quite unnecessary – they had been married for years. They moved in at about the same time as us, and they were already married back then. Couldn't he have kept all that whispering to the bedroom? They didn't have any children after all – maybe because of what he'd been getting up to.

He must have been worried his wife would come barging

in. He couldn't very well lock the door, because that would have made her suspicious straight away. Just imagine if she pushed open the door and caught him at it. No use her backing out of the room. No use him covering up. There was no getting out of this one. He'd had it. It would have been less embarrassing to have a bad fall, or to go bankrupt, or even to get hacked to death. This was worse than dying – at least if he died his wife might miss him. But if she caught him wanking it would be a stain he could never erase. His wife wouldn't punish him. There would just be a wall of silence. He wouldn't even know if she still remembered. Fuck! Was this man so desperate for a wank that he was prepared to risk everything?

I began to pay more attention to what was going on upstairs. Everything was heavy with significance: a tiny vibration, a clunk, the click of a door shutting, the smell of hot cooking oil, of rice wine being poured into the pan. I followed every minute detail and was delighted at even the slightest clue about their movements, gloating at my secret knowledge. Their footsteps were quite different, one a slow, heavy tread, the other light and quick with the sharp rap of high heels – these were obviously the wife's. She moved around a lot more too, going from the bedroom to the kitchen, and from the kitchen to the sitting room. Her chores were never-ending. Eventually the footsteps would stop, with a clop, and another clop, as first one shoe then the other dropped to the floor by the bed. The sounds faded into the quietness of the night, but still I listened. I imagined them in bed, him stifling a yawn to show how tired he was. Night-night, turn out the light. Nothing doing tonight. It was deathly quiet. I kept listening. I couldn't sleep, didn't dare sleep, I was afraid of missing anything. I forced myself to stay awake. Then in the early dawn, the sounds upstairs started again. She started by the bed, then went to the bathroom. The toilet flushed, then she came out and went to the kitchen – I imagined her bleary eyed – and started clattering pots and bowls. She was alone. I knew where he was: behind the thinnest of plywood doors, playing with himself.

Did she have any idea what he was up to in their bed? It must still have held the warmth of her body, the scent of her perfume, maybe even a strand or two of her hair. Did she have the slightest suspicion?

Once I tried to catch him at it. I went up and knocked on the door. She opened it in her nightgown, obviously surprised to see me. I had to come up with some pretext, so I said 'There's water dripping from your balcony.'

'No, there isn't.' she said, even more surprised. I gave her a sceptical look. 'We haven't washed it down,' she added, opening the door a bit wider, as if asking me to see for myself.

At last I was in the home I had spent so much time wondering about. Was that a whiff of semen? The dining area was in the corner of the sitting room, as I had guessed, on the north side. There was a plate of toast on the dining room table – those clunks must have been the toaster. And the floors were parquet – no wonder I could hear everything so clearly. The bedroom door was made of Manchurian ash ply. It was shut, but I knew what was going on behind those flimsy panels. I couldn't believe I was so close to exposing him. But she held back. Then I realised that you had to go through the bedroom to get to the balcony – what a brilliant excuse I had come up with.

'If you want to sluice down the balcony, can you just let

us know?' I said. 'Then we can put our stuff away. We've hung things out to dry downstairs.'

'But we didn't,' she protested. 'My husband's still asleep.'

Huh! I thought to myself. Some sleep.

She went back into the kitchen and carried on making breakfast. She lit the gas and broke two eggs into the frying pan.

'We were late to bed last night.' She sounded embarrassed. She came back wiping her hands on the dishcloth as if she was the maid. She looked like a complete innocent, so vulnerable. She had absolutely no idea. I had a sudden urge to lunge at the bedroom door and kick it open. There he'd be in the throes of ecstasy, his penis standing up straight, semen pearling on the tip like snot. The veil would be torn from her eyes. She'd be shocked to discover she'd been living a lie, she might even try to kill herself in a frenzy of despair. The idea brought me up short. At that moment, she shouted and rushed back to the kitchen. She grabbed the smoking frying pan in a panic and lifted it high above the hob, where the gas still flamed. She didn't know what to do, just looked at me for help.

'Sorry, but would you pass me that?' she said, waving at the spatula.

The pans, brushes and other utensils hung neatly from a row of hooks on the wall. Her doing, no doubt. I thought I was going to cry. I took down the spatula and passed it to her. She reached out a long, bony hand and took it from me.

'Burnt food gives you cancer.' She turned the eggs out. 'He always sleeps late, otherwise you could sit and wait for him to wake up.'

Chen Xiwo

2

I fled. I just didn't have the courage to wait until he came out. I would be dragging him from the world of his secret pleasure to face this wife of his, a wife who was in complete ignorance of what he was doing. It would be too cruel.

'It must be the people upstairs,' I said.

'We'd never do that,' she said as she saw me out. 'We wouldn't be so antisocial.'

I nodded. Then – so as not to wreck my story – I went upstairs and knocked and asked if there was water dripping from their balcony.

I was starting to feel sorry for her. Every time I saw her, I thought of what her husband was up to. Because of him, her body carried the smell of it. Did she lie awake at night and stare into the darkness, filled with disappointment because something was missing in her life? The worst thing was that she probably didn't know what was wrong. She had no idea her husband was giving another woman what he should have been giving to her, giving it to the woman of his fantasies.

Masturbation is like driving – all men masturbate at one time or another, just like everybody breaks the law when they drive. I used to have dark fantasies about doing impossible things to a girl I didn't know. But as soon I got married I stopped, because I believed that husband and wife have certain obligations to each other in that department. Either

30

both should be getting it, or neither. If one enjoyed pleasure and not the other, that was a betrayal. There was too much unfaithfulness nowadays, especially among people like him. Of course I didn't really know what he did, but he looked like he had his own business and one day I heard a visitor call him 'Boss'. There are plenty of women in this world ready to play the whore and drop their knickers for their boss.

Not that I had strong feelings either way about whores. They were part of life in our city, just like the air we breathed. When you invited guests to a restaurant, you naturally had a few hostesses there, for a bit of fun. Once everyone demanded that a hostess show us her tits, and she did. Everyone laughed. I laughed too. Really it was no big deal. It's what they do. They're hostesses, just like we're company bosses. That's just the way we do business.

One evening I was wining and dining a business contact I met through my friend, Water. He got his nickname because he spreads it around so often that we all say his spunk must be thin as water. It was because of Water that I started selling health tonics and supplements – he saved me.

Before I met Water, I'd been running around like a headless chicken, with nothing more than a mock leather briefcase, selling anything from chemicals to watermelons. I had just graduated and wanted to start a whole new life: I was willing to run, I was willing to graft. I was educated, but I'd still been fooled. I had just done my biggest deal ever – a truck full of Hami melons from Xinjiang – but the buyer had vanished and the melons were rotting in front of my eyes. I rushed to the place where the buyer worked, but he had taken time off and no one knew where he'd gone. Just then Water turned up like a man rescuing a drowning dog, and sold some of the melons for me.

'In this world,' he said, 'you're better off selling than making, and selling fake brands is best of all.' That was my moment of enlightenment.

Our guest that night was the deputy head of the provincial hospital. We were going to book some hostesses but he didn't want to. So we didn't. Though I could have done with it. I was really tense – I don't know why.

Since he didn't want women, we just plied him with food and drink. But he said he couldn't hold his drink, so he didn't want much of that either.

Several times I tried to start a conversation about how the hospital bought drugs, but the deputy head was having none of it.

'Are you trying to give me the hard sell?' he said.

'Of course not,' we protested.

'Medicines are vital to human life,' he intoned.

'Yes, but drugs can kill you,' Water replied. 'Our tonics and supplements are totally harmless.'

Having no hostesses to propose the toasts was worse than having an empty table.

'Let's go to the sauna,' said Water.

The deputy head wasn't keen on that idea either, but Water insisted.

'You have so many important matters to attend to every day, Mr Zhou, you need a chance to take it easy.'

He certainly knew what to say. Of course, normally so would I, but for some reason I was awkward that night.

After we had got to the sauna and stripped off, the deputy head finally began to relax and talk about the ups and downs of his job. Heading up a hospital was hard, he said, he'd much rather have an easy-going job like mine.

'Well, today you can relax too,' said Water.'You can have a massage.'

Zhou just laughed and said nothing, so Water rushed off to ask the manager if they had any pretty masseusses.

'All our masseuses are pretty,' declared the manager, gesturing to the girls sitting and lying and strolling around the dimly-lit rooms. They certainly did look attractive.

'We want the best-looking,' said Water.

'Of course.' The manager smirked. 'Nothing but the best for bosses like you.'

'He's the big boss,' said Water, pointing at me. 'You don't want to mess with someone like him.' I didn't like Water saying that one bit.

We trooped along to pick our girls. Zhou was playing coy, but when he smiled at one of the girls Water took the hint and called her out. He was quite straightforward about it, beckoning her over with his finger. Had I ever summoned a girl like that?

When it came to my turn, I said I'd pass. Water grabbed my arm.

'What the hell's up with you?' he hissed. 'Don't leave me out on a limb.'

Sure enough, our guest said he'd pass too.

'That's not what I meant,' I added hurriedly. 'I just want to go to the toilet first.'

'Of course,' said the manager. 'But please choose your girl first, sir, and she'll wait for you in the cubicle.'

'Don't call me sir, I'm not the big boss,' I said.

They led us down a discreet inner corridor, past dimly-lit cubicles furnished with identical massage beds. There was a stale smell of cologne and cosmetics – I could hardly breathe. The girl's hair reeked of grease and tobacco. Soon I did, too. Two hard-soft lumps were resting on my head while she massaged my face, though their owner didn't seem to notice. My heightened senses could pick out the lines on the tips of her fingers, the moisturiser oozing in and out of the whorls. She was dissecting my soul with a warm scalpel, like meat on a chopping board. I couldn't understand how I'd found all this relaxing before.

She reached down to my chest and tweaked my nipples.

'Why do you always do that?' I'd never thought to ask.

'Why not?' she replied. 'The male chest is very sensitive.'

'No, that's not what I meant.'

'Just tell me if it feels good, sir. That's the important thing.'

Her smile was poppy red, obscene. I grabbed her hand and held it away from my body.

'No more massage, let's just talk,' I said.

I asked her where she came from and how old she was. Her hands kept stroking me.

'No more massage,' I said again. She stopped.

'What kind of business are you in?' she asked.

'I'm not in business.'

Her hands twitched. She couldn't keep them still. She was supposed to be working. This was her job. Her hands were warm. I couldn't bear it any more. I jerked away.

'No … more … massage!' I shouted.

The hands went limp as if they were dead. The girl was shocked – she had no idea what she'd done wrong. There were footsteps outside and she burst into floods of tears. Maybe I had gone too far. I got up, opened the door and went out. The people who'd gathered in the corridor drifted away. The manager rushed up and put a hand on my arm.

'Please tell me, sir, how the girl has failed to attend to your needs.'

'Failed to attend to my needs? She attended a bit too much!'

The manager pushed past me into the cubicle and shouted at the girl: 'What have you done to our guest?'

'Nothing!' she protested. He turned back to me.

'What's the matter, sir? We do proper massage here!'

'He didn't want a massage … ' said the girl.

'You didn't want a massage?' the manager shouted. 'So what are you doing here? Did you come to the wrong place? Are you crazy?'

Maybe I was crazy, though I'd never had any trouble before. Some of the girls were giving me funny looks. Just then our guest came out, still doing up the belt to his trousers. He pretended not to see me. Water was there too, looking horrified. I could understand why – I knew what my little scene would do for our business with the provincial hospital. What I didn't know was why I had done it. All I knew was that I couldn't bear that place any more. I was contaminated. I had to get out of there, I had to go somewhere clean.

I went home. The kid was asleep and my wife was folding the quilts. They were piled all over the sitting room chairs. The light was very bright, glaring off the cotton covers. Was this really my home? I had no idea we owned so many quilts – our sitting room looked like a warehouse. I panicked, I couldn't breathe. My wife said something to me but I didn't hear what it was. She carried a quilt out of the room, holding it against her stomach so she looked pregnant. The corner brushed against me and I backed away … and trod on something. The floor was covered in Lego and grubby old dolls. My wife spoke again. She seemed to be asking if I was hungry. I didn't answer, just went into the bathroom and shut the door, overwhelmed by a strange feeling of emptiness. The smell of cosmetics, cologne and moisturiser clung to me faintly, like a distant memory. After I had stood there for a while, my wife knocked on the door, came in, hitched up her nightie and sat down to pee. Just like that. Right in front of me. It felt like a bad joke, as if I was a voyeur. I suppose I shouldn't have felt like that. After all, she was my wife. But it was disgusting. I left the bathroom and got into bed. It was cold as ice, strange. I wanted the light off. I could only find peace in darkness.

3

My phone rang. It was Water.

'What's up with you, mate?' he said.

'What do you mean, what's up?' But I knew just what he meant.

He laughed.

'Are you so in love that massage parlours make you feel dirty?'

'Huh! Who would I be in love with? Love's a losing game … '

'Don't go telling me it's because your wife's so beautiful,' he said.'However beautiful your wife is, she's still your wife, and you're going to get tired of her eventually. You can't

36

stick to the same dish your whole life, can you?'

'Piss off.'

'Besides, the very fact you chose yourself such a hot wife shows that you're a randy bastard.' He was laying it on thick.

'You think those hookers were so attractive?' I glanced nervously in the direction of the bathroom. 'Leave me alone. I'm going to sleep.'

'Who with?' Water wasn't giving up easily.

'Fuck off,' I said. 'You want to get tested for HIV, mate.'

There was a burst of laughter from the other end of the phone.

'Better die getting some than stay alive and not get any.'

I could hear my wife's footsteps. I put down the phone and turned off the light.

How many men were still out there, screwing around in bars and massage parlours? There were any number of places to go to. How many men were having sex with women who weren't their wives at that very minute? How many men started the night in another woman's arms and finished it lying beside their wives? Weren't they worried the other woman would see them one day, walking down the street with their wife? What would the other woman think of her? Poor wives, they didn't know they were sharing their husband's penis – revolting – like sharing a toothbrush. They had no idea, no idea where they'd picked up that embarrassing infection. They probably thought they'd caught it off a public toilet.

The woman living upstairs was always going up and down in the lifts with bags – shopping on the way up, rubbish on the way down. They had so much rubbish because they bought so much stuff. They must have been addicted to the consumer lifestyle. When I was taking the lift, I would watch her in the mirror as we descended. She was always so demure. I never struck up a conversation. The bags of rubbish were so heavy she had to struggle to drag them across to the bins.

'It must be heavy for her,' I said.

'Who?' my wife asked. I hadn't seen her come in.

'The couple upstairs. She does everything in their house.'

'What's it got to do with you?' asked my wife.

'Her husband takes her for granted.'

'You should pay more attention to your own family,' said my wife. 'Where shall we go and eat this weekend?'

Going out to eat was our weekend ritual. Home cooking had lost its appeal, we ate the same old things in the same old ways – fried or steamed, skinned or whole, spicy or plain. So at weekends we ate out. We ate all sorts of Chinese regional delicacies. Then we tried foreign food – Kentucky Fried Chicken, McDonald's, a steak dinner or Japanese. But none of it was really satisfying. We even tried Korean teppanyaki, where you can watch the cooks at work and have a go yourself, but it soon palled.

'Anywhere,' I said.

'Where do you mean, anywhere?'

'Let's not bother.'

'Why ever not?' she yelped. I'd never said anything like this before.

'I'm busy,' I said. Being busy was always a man's best excuse.

'Busy? You're not too busy to watch the TV.' She grabbed the remote off me.

'You don't know what just happened.'

'What happened?' She sounded worried.

38

'There's no point in telling you.' I wanted to change the subject.

'Then it's obviously nothing.'

'You're so infuriating!' I flared up. Something had happened – but what? 'You've got it too easy,' I carried on. 'You never even notice the people upstairs.'

'What's wrong with them? I saw them out on their stroll today, as usual.'

'What's it got to do with going out for a stroll? It's all fake!' I shouted. 'You should feel sorry for her.'

'Why don't you feel sorry for me?'

The conversation was heading in an alarming direction, so I tried to calm her down. 'Let's ask the kid where we should go and eat.'

It was kind of ridiculous – my daughter was only three. As soon as she heard me talking about her she piped up 'Mum! I want Natrol Sleep Restore!' She was watching the Natrol advert on TV, the jingle warbling 'The only gift for Mum and Dad is Natrol Sleep Restore!'

'Let's go and have monkey brains,' I said.

'Sure,' said my wife. 'I saw that leaflet too. A Manchu Han Imperial Feast monkey brain soup.'

I knew all about weird food fads. Chinese people have so much faith in supplements: kidney tonics for men, blood tonics for women, calcium for the old folks, brain supplements for the kids. Once someone tried to persuade me to buy a brain supplement called Monkey Spirit. He showed me some soft stuff which he claimed, in all seriousness, was monkey brain. I told him it might as well be pig brain for all I knew. People went for stuff like that because they were desperate. If I had dementia and someone told me pig brain would help

I'd believe them just as much, because I had no choice.

I waited in the car for my wife and daughter to get ready, starting the engine, cutting it, starting it up again. I was trying to be patient, like a good husband and father. I smacked the steering wheel. Finally they appeared, my wife straightening my daughter's sash with one hand, and buttoning her fashionable coat with the other. She started dabbing at the mask of make-up caked on her face, anxious to eliminate the slightest flaw.

'What are you doing?' I asked. 'We're not going to an exhibition, we're going out to eat.' Almost shouting the word 'eat'.

Dad at the wheel, Mum in the passenger seat, our daughter squeezed in between. That was how we did it when we went out. The child jogged my arm with her elbow – my wife tried to get her to move over a little.

We hadn't even gone a kilometre when we had to stop so my daughter could do a pee. Then we had to stop again so my wife could buy some cough sweets. She stuffed one into my mouth. I said I didn't want one.

'But you always want one,' said my wife.

'I just don't want one now.'

'Suck a sweet, Daddy, suck a sweet,' my daughter joined in.

This was all too much. How had I ever put up with them before? When I first bought it, I thought the car would make me free, but instead I had to cart around all this baggage. Water was right. He only used his car for going on trips with his girlfriends. If I called him on the phone he'd always say he was out of town in Beijing, or Shanghai, or Shenzhen, or even in the States.

'Damn it, which girl are you with now?' I'd ask. 'You're

sleeping all over the place.'

He'd roar with laughter.

'Jealous, huh. You can fuck anywhere, you know. Even inside a car.'

This wasn't the kind of high-end, haute cuisine restaurant I normally go to. There were grotesque piles of jagged rocks all over the room. The diners were all on their feet at one table, cheering and pushing and shoving to get a better look in the dim light. It was like some primitive scene of slaughter.

'What are they looking at?' asked my daughter.

'I don't know,' I said. I had a good idea but I didn't want to let on straight away.

The waiter took us to a row of cages so we could choose our monkey. The victims knew what we were up to and started gibbering defiantly. Maybe this was all a necessary part of the process. One of the beasts gave a diabolical screech, so I said we'd have him. As the lad reached into the cage, all the other monkeys scrabbled away, pushing ours to the front. Our monkey turned around and tried to squeeze back into the group like a coward, sticking its bright red rump up at us. But that just made us roar with laughter. Then I spotted another monkey, a big fine fellow, right at the back in prime position, and I changed my mind.

'Let's have that big strong one instead,' I said.

They took us to a luxurious side room, done out entirely in silk like a huge, soft bed. In the middle of the dining table was a hole for the monkey's head, a sign of the bloodbath to come. I felt a throb of excitement. I heard another cheer from the dining room, and a chilling screech – more drama. Was their monkey fiercer than ours, or was it protesting because it was first for the chop?

Chen Xiwo

Our monkey arrived in chains, with the top of its head shaved smooth. They'd given it a wash, but it was still scratching and covered with fleas. The waiters handed me a saw and a hammer made from silver, then shoved the monkey under the table and clamped a vice around its neck so the head stuck through the hole. Its eyes flickered over the three of us, full of fear. Monkeys are much more intelligent than other animals. It knew just what was coming – that was what made it so exciting. My wife pulled on my arm. It wasn't like her to be so physical. She always used words if she wanted something, like asking me to tuck the quilt in around our daughter on my side of the bed.

I paid no attention. I didn't even look at her, just brushed her off. I didn't look at the monkey either. I wanted it to be in limbo, like a prisoner who can feel the gun jabbing into the back of his head, but has no idea when the shot will be fired. That's real fear. I've felt it too.

I lifted the hammer. I brought it down hard. The monkey screeched, but the blow wasn't hard enough to crack the skull. I tried again, but only made a small crack. My daughter shrieked in terror, as if she had finally realised what was happening. My wife put her hands in front of my daughter's eyes. A smile spread over my face. I was trying to figure out how to split open the monkey's skull. The skull was hard – the monkey was big and strong, which made the prospect of eating its brains all the more enticing. I picked up the silver saw, shoved it into the crack and pried the skull open. The monkey gave a blood-curdling scream. At last I could see its brain. It was smooth, with a slickness that seemed barbaric, completely at odds with our gentle, civilised world. It throbbed. My daughter shrieked in fear again. Let her. She

42

needed to understand fear. She'd had life too easy.

'Shriek all you like,' I told her. 'It can't escape and now we're going to eat its brain.'

The waiter came over and asked whether we wanted it raw or poached at the table in a spicy soup. Both were good for longevity, he continued. It was tasty in a soup, but if you ate it raw, it was particularly nutritious. I asked my wife which she preferred, but she sat there, shaking.

'It's just food,' I said. 'What did you think we were going to do?'

I told the waiter we'd have them raw, with a hot dressing. The oil sizzled as he poured it – the monkey gave a lurch, its face suddenly old and wizened.

'Eat!' I said, and dug in with a serving spoon. The brains wobbled on the spoon. Then it was between my teeth. It was struggling, struggling between my teeth. It was good, better than I had ever imagined with the monkey alive like this, struggling in pain and screeching in despair. But I felt empty. There was a cavity in a corner of the monkey's skull. I could feel the pain of that emptiness, the same pain as having a tooth drilled, or when something hits a nerve, the pain of hunger which needs something to fill it. Maybe I should fight pain with pain. Or spoon out some more brains. That was what the animal wanted. I drew the spoon gently along the edge of the gash in its skull, imagining, deep inside me, the echo of the pain I was causing.

'Eat!' I yelled at my wife. She was still shaking. She took our daughter in her arms and turned away. I brandished the spoon, but I didn't know whether to scoop out another mouthful or not. If I stopped eating I'd lose control of the situation, but if I carried on I would end the creature's suffering and that would be no good to me.

I wanted to see its face. I bent down. The monkey bared its teeth in a grin. I hadn't expected that either. I couldn't figure out the connection between a smile and pain.

I felt utterly useless.

I wanted to make it bite me.

I jabbed with the spoon, jabbed and stirred. A thudding came from under the table, like the hooves of a galloping horse. I yelled at my wife again, but she still wouldn't eat. I dug out a spoonful and held it in front of her mouth. She shook her head, her mouth tight shut.

'What are you doing here if you don't want to eat?' I shouted.

'I didn't know it would be like this,' she wailed, shaking her head.

'How did you think it would be?'

'I'm not having any!' she yelled back.

She knocked the spoon out of my hand, spattering monkey brains on the floor. It was like soft tofu.

'Do you think this is cheap?' I don't know why I brought up money, it wasn't as if we were short of it. 'Eat! Go on – eat!'

I gouged out some more brains and tried to prise open her mouth, but she kept it clamped shut. The monkey brains quivering on the spoon were smeared with her lipstick, a fake, lurid red. There was monkey brains smeared on her lips and cheek as well. She was all spotty. She disgusted me. I mean, it was just eating, wasn't it? Don't you eat every day? Three times a day … Eating live fish and shrimp and all that doesn't bother you, does it? And this is dead monkey, just a corpse, you're just eating a corpse! A corpse!

Suddenly my wife threw up. I was furious.

'Now look at you!' I shouted.

4

Normally, my wife looked impeccable. She was still one of the best-looking women on our block. But at that moment she wasn't looking pretty at all. She looked as rough as a salted ribbon fish.

Loads of men used to be after her. I was always afraid, when we were going out, that one of them would snatch her away from me. Right up until we married, she was getting phone calls from other men, but in the end she chose me. She was a sensible woman, and if she couldn't do something properly, she didn't do it at all. Perfect wife material.

After we married, everything about her, like her pretty face, solidified. I earned the money and she managed it – our life was like a train chugging along the same old track, day after day. I started slumping down on the sofa or snuggling up in the duvet and watching TV, wearing out the remote, even though I never wanted to watch anything. I put on weight. Sometimes I even hoped that some rival would appear, to rekindle the frantic desire I used to feel when I feared someone might steal her away from me.

As soon as I had graduated, reality hit. I needed to earn proper money if I was going to get a wife. I used to go around with my briefcase, begging favours, making what I could from buying and selling chemicals. I told my wife that a stash of money I happened to come by was actually a regular monthly salary. I don't know what I would have said to her if I hadn't finally started selling tonics and supplements. I yearned to possess her body, come what may.

Now that body belonged wholly to me, lay in bed next to me, but it didn't make my heart skip a beat. Now she could change her clothes in front of me, wash the bra and panties she had stripped off and hang them out to dry on the balcony – and I was unmoved.

We had become lazy about our love life. I would invariably be on top, and everything – the speed of my thrusts, how long I kept going – was always just the same. We just couldn't be bothered with each other. We'd look at the grandfather clock which stood at the end of the bed and the minute hand would leap forward – it always leaped forward, whenever you looked at it. Then we'd turn to each other in surprise and start yawning.

'Is it really so late?'

'Time to go to sleep.'

'Yup.'

And we'd switch off the light.

We knew what the other was thinking. We were both terrified that some day one of us would see through the pretence. The clock was only in the bedroom – standing there like a coffin – to give us an excuse as soon as we got into bed. That tick-tock, it was hypnotic. It put you to sleep, lulled you into carrying on living just as you always had.

One look, one leap of the minute hand.

But you don't want to do it too often. A couple of times a week is all right. Monday, Wednesday and Friday, or Tuesday, Thursday and Saturday, like my parents' political study classes in the Cultural Revolution. Or maybe only twice a week – you have to look after your body. Early to bed, early to rise and early morning exercise … it's important to have good habits. But it's the bad habits that keep you going: staying up late, sleeping in, smoking, drinking, fighting with the wife, playing mah-jong, flirting and having affairs …

We only ever talked about stupid, insignificant things. Today I saw so and so. What's more nutritious: eggs that are cooked through or only half-cooked? Who's won top prize in the lottery. Wasn't that university student who poured acid over a bear just appalling? China's won the bid for the Olympics. Let's buy a villa …

We all make up hot topics, we invent illusions. We kid our daughter that she can get into a top university and go abroad to study, we kid girls and boys that they can look like glamorous stars, we kid lovers that sentimental tosh is real love, we kid grown ups that they can succeed in business and lead a life of luxury, we kid women that they can stay eternally young and beautiful, we kid old folks they can enjoy long, healthy lives, we kid the frail that they can be strong. Even the modernisation of China is just a myth. It's not just the biggest myth of all, it's a factory for churning out myths: science and technology are progressing by leaps and bounds, life is getting better and better, we're doing really well, and, hey, we're going to need the strongest anti-theft locks … But when one of us comes back home, the other doesn't even bother to turn around, they just wait for the key to turn in the lock. Who else could it be anyway? Even the door swings open lazily.

But one day the door opened and a strange woman was standing there. No shit. This woman – this intruder – had long, straight hair. She wafted into the room, bold as brass, and I leaped up from the sofa.

'You know what this is?' asks my wife. She always had curly hair, ever since I first knew her. It was her crowning glory.

'No,' I said.

'It's a straight perm. Guess how much it cost. 800 yuan.'

'Wow, big spender.'

It was very odd. There was a strange woman in my kitchen, using my wok and my ladle, wringing out my dishcloths, opening my fridge, gliding to and fro. When she brought food to the table, all I could see was a curtain of straight hair. Her face was hidden, her body enveloped in a faint, medicinal smell. I couldn't stop watching her as she darted into the sitting room and straightened the cushions on the sofa, as she got some women's underwear out of the bedroom closet and floated into the bathroom. I pretended I needed a piss and went in too. But as I was unzipping my trousers I stopped – I didn't dare to in front of this strange woman. I went back into the sitting room, leaving the bathroom door ajar, and listened uneasily to the sound of the shower. I crept back to the bathroom and pushed the door a little further open. Her body was naked beneath the dark waterfall of her hair. She stepped into the bath. My bath. I looked round at the bathroom with new eyes. That bath towel had only just been wrapped around her body. That shower gel was just about to be smeared all over it. I hardly dared look. I couldn't leave. I slowly crept forwards. She was facing the other way. For the first time in a long while my head swam and my heart pounded. I shut my eyes and pounced. The water poured over my face as we leaned forwards. I held her in a wet embrace.

She struggled a bit but soon submitted and allowed me to knead her all over. She started to moan. An unusual sound. An unusual position. A mane of hair, like a horse.

'Hang on a minute,' she said. 'Wait for me in bed.'

Maybe we'd wanted a child so we didn't have to confront all this. Maybe this was the reason we'd had a daughter as well. I remember reading in a book that when a woman has to orgasm to produce the alkalinity which lets her conceive a son. What about me? Orgasms, maybe, but not much excitement.

We stopped being lovers as soon as our daughter was born. We were just Mum and Dad loving our child together. Life was terrifyingly full of her crying, fussing, milk, porridge, tins of this and that, peeing, pooing and nappies. I earned the money for the child, my wife fed her. I drove the car for the child, she changed her nappy. I was the one who tucked in the right-hand side of the child's quilt, she tucked in the left-hand side.

Where had all my semen gone over the years? It must have seeped away into the innumerable capillaries along my vas deferens. I'd never played away with other women, or even had wet dreams, although I used to worry about it. The embarrassment of stains on the sheets. I used to worry about the lack of sex, and sometimes thought I should sort myself out. If I got some toilet paper ready I could probably do it without making a mess. But in the end I didn't. So where had all my sperm gone?

I sneaked back into the building opposite. My footsteps echoed in the empty building, the traces of my last visit still clear in the thick dust. I turned off my mobile. It was like hiding in an abandoned well. A burst of noise from people passing in the street below, then silence fell again, deeper than before. I was alone. As usual, the woman opposite was busy in her kitchen – they took a lot of trouble over their food. She was in her nightie, all skin and bones, exploited, bled dry, like depleted soil. Sometimes I wished she had a lover – it was only what her husband deserved – but there was no sign of one. She taught at a medical school nearby. I used to spot her coming out of a classroom, pale and drawn, but I never saw her talking to any of her colleagues. She never smiled. She was timid, like a sheep, holding her teaching notes close to her chest, as if hiding her scrawny bosom. She didn't have many friends. The only one I saw was an elegant nurse who went around with her hand tucked into the pocket of her uniform.

Something was bubbling on the stove. She took off the lid and steam billowed out, rounding out her figure. She was very much at home in her kitchen, her movements practised, deft. She took a ladle and filled a very small bowl from the pot – the broth must have been very precious. She tasted it and then carried the bowl into the sitting room. He was sitting up at the table for dinner, but when she gave him the bowl, he didn't want it. He pushed the bowl back to her, but she wouldn't take it either. They argued as it went back and forth until she picked it up and headed for the bathroom to throw it down the toilet. He came after her and tried to grab it, but now she wouldn't give it up. He started pleading, begging her. He certainly could put on an act. Finally she allowed herself to be persuaded. She made a playful fist and punched him gently on the shoulder. He smiled. Would she have been making jokes if she had known the lie that lay behind his smile? Would she have cooked for him at all?

But we're all hypocrites. That's something the empty flat

50

taught me. There were plenty of other scenes to watch when our upstairs neighbours weren't at home. It was non-stop entertainment. The woman in the next flat spent all her time putting on make up and admiring herself in the mirror. On the other side was an old boy who was forever groping his live-in housekeeper. She'd just carry on with whatever she was doing as if nothing was happening. Once I saw her leading him out on to the street – he must have been unwell – supporting him by the arm like a dutiful granddaughter while she called him a cab. The boy in the flat downstairs used to spend all day hiding in his parents' bedroom watching TV – changing the channel as soon as his parents got back. One man on the ninth floor used to practise fierce expressions, nodding and jerking his eyebrows up and down like a yoyo. Once I thought he flashed me a smile, but he couldn't see me, he was just smiling at himself. An old woman on the fifth floor was always in bed, fiddling with a radio and paying no attention to her children when they went in and out of her room. Once they organised a party to celebrate her reaching one hundred years old. Everyone said she'd reached such a great age because her family took such good care of her. But a few days later she struggled out of bed, staggered to the window and scrambled awkwardly on to the ledge, wailing like a cat.

'I don't want to live any more,' she screeched.

Her son and daughter grabbed her and held on.

'Oh, please don't make such a fuss,' they begged. 'Whatever will the neighbours think? Haven't we done enough for you?'

Eventually the old woman climbed back in. She would have to go on enduring pain and misery so her children could keep up the pretence of her blessed old age. Her home was her living hell.

Our upstairs neighbour was in the kitchen again, wearing her nightie. It hung so loosely on her that it seemed to swathe her like a parcel. She looked preoccupied as I watched her body moving under its wrappings, her bosom, her soft waist, the slopes and creases of her belly and hips. Her husband was there too – he rarely seemed to go out. Why wasn't he entertaining clients? What was a grown man doing with himself, stuck at home all evening?

They were talking. He followed her around the house, from kitchen to sitting room, whispering into her ear. He went everywhere with her. But I wanted her to be free of his shadow. I only wanted to see her. Time edged by. He was still following her every move. Hypocrite! Stop being such a fake. I know what you're going to do as soon as you get into bed.

Eventually they got ready for bed. She stood there in her nightie. The light went off. Everything died. Darkness. I stared into the darkness. My mind started to wander. I stared. Slowly my hand went down to my crotch. I knew what I was going to do. I imagined that body in that bed. I could imagine anything, do anything. Like an emperor. My dreams were so much more seductive than reality.

Then she sat up.

What was she doing?

All I could see was her silhouette ...

5

I got some night vision binoculars off the black market. That wasn't a problem – I was used to picking things up illegally – but then I realised I had no place to keep them. I wasn't that bothered about losing them, but I didn't want my secret getting out.

I couldn't store them in my safe at work, any one of the staff might get a crowbar and walk off with them. It wasn't safe to leave them in the car, there were far too many thieves around. And I certainly couldn't bring them home. None of our drawers was locked. They all had keys, but god knows where the keys had got to. And I couldn't change the locks. How could I explain a drawer which suddenly had to be kept locked?

I'd never had any secrets. I didn't even have my own money. My wife and my daughter could rifle through all the drawers as much as they wanted. How stupid. I should have kept some privacy.

There was nothing in the world that was only mine.

Then it occurred to me I could hide the binoculars in the space above the dropped ceiling. Not in the sitting room – how would I ever get them in or out without someone seeing? – but in the bathroom. The bathroom was right by the front door as well.

I went to the toilet, locked the door, turned on the tap,

took out a ceiling panel and stowed the binoculars away. I couldn't help smiling as I came out. I'd never been this secretive before, not even when I was selling fake drugs.

Our city was famous as China's biggest centre of herbal medicine. Secret imperial remedies, age-old prescriptions, the Yellow Emperor's medical encyclopedia, the theories of yin and yang and the five processes, everyone could spout them chapter and verse. Our city was also notorious for having its very own 'Bin Laden', a gangster who always dealt ruthlessly with his enemies. I'd seen him cut someone's liver out to use for medicine with my own eyes. Right there in the street. His thugs grabbed hold of his victim, and he brought the knife down with a swish, as if it were a calligraphy brush. The man begged for mercy. Bin Laden listened. He asked questions. It looked like they were negotiating. The victim seemed calm as Bin Laden slowly drew a line down his chest, as if he was being tickled and holding back a laugh. Suddenly the knife thrust in and blood spurted out, spattering the bystanders. Bin Laden stepped aside. The murdered man lay still, uncomprehending, as if he was trying to smile. The colour drained from his face. The blood pooled on the ground. His liver was still warm. It had taken less than three minutes.

In the end, Bin Laden fell victim himself to a government crackdown.

The day of his execution, people swarmed to see him. As they dragged Bin Laden from the prison truck, the crowd went wild. They surged forward shaking their fists and shouting.

'Shooting's too good for him!'

'Death by a thousand cuts!'

'Dig out his kidney and eat it!'

The police were losing control. They fired shots in the

air, but nobody took any notice, so they linked arms to keep the crowd back. Someone threw a stone at Bin Laden. He jerked his head and glared around him. There was a stunned silence. Then a child standing towards the back shouted 'Bin Laden's still alive!'

The crowd stampeded forwards ...

I hadn't seen Water since the day I'd stormed out of the massage parlour, a lifetime ago. When he came over to my house he didn't even mention it, just started bragging about how many chicks he'd laid – or eaten, as he put it.

'You're such a loser,' I said.

'Not like you. You've got a chick that's not even a chick. Classy.'

I was taken aback, but gave him a smile.

'I haven't "eaten" her.'

'No. She's just your sex object.' My heart missed a beat. 'Love is sex, and sex is all about the imagination,' Water continued. 'After all, what's so exciting about a lump of meat?'

'You talk a load of crap.'

'The world is vast and we should have the imaginations to find our heart's desires and leap over any walls we want,' he said. 'But let me offer you a bit of advice: however many walls you jump over, mind you guard the wall of your own home.'

I was shocked.

'Don't listen to the rubbish my wife says.'

'I'm right, aren't I?' He laughed. 'Look, we're old mates, there isn't much we don't know about each other. Your wife hasn't found out your secret yet, so take your chance while you can, and live the good life. Live to steal, steal to live ... '

'For god's sake! If you've got something to say, damn

well spit it out!'

'Here's something I can't hide from you.' He gave me a sly smile, as if we were partners in crime. I didn't like this one bit. 'Want to do a bit of business?'

'What?'

'Kidneys.'

'Not kidney tonics again? What is it this time? Yan Nian Tonic, Hui Yuan Tonic? Viagra?' I teased him.

'Bin Laden's kidney,' he said, drawing his finger across his neck.

I almost jumped out of my skin.

'Bin Laden's kidney is worth a fortune. Did you see him after he'd been executed, eyes still glaring like a tiger?'

'It'd be easier to sell a dog's kidney.' I smiled. 'But this is a man's kidney. Are you going to open up a hospital? Do transplants?'

'I knew you wouldn't understand. We don't need any hospital. What's the point of a hospital anyway? A "public" service. However much money there is swilling round the system, it always goes to someone else. You got to do a deal like this outside the system. That way, you can keep all the profit for yourself.'

'I suppose you can name any price you want,' I said, 'there's plenty of money around. I'll fix you up with a dialysis machine.'

'What are you talking about?' he shouted. 'They just eat it.'

I thought I was going to be sick.

'What – are you scared?'

'Get lost' I said.

'Don't worry, it's totally safe. It'll go on their health insurance, a special deal.'

'Get lost,' I said again.

'What's up with you?'

'Fuck off.'

In all my years of selling tonics and supplements, I'd dreamed up all sorts of scams. I'd palmed off pig brains as monkey brains and field mushrooms as cancer-beating lingzhi mushrooms. I'd mixed tonic wine with wood alcohol, and made pills from flour. I'd even tried to sell people human urine and menstrual blood. But eating a human kidney – a kidney taken from a healthy human body – had never even crossed my mind. Where had this remedy come from? There must have been some secret imperial recipe, handed down through the generations. Or maybe I had let things slip, and new trends had passed me by. I had only ever heard of robbing organs from dead bodies in hospital. I'd never heard of stealing them from condemned criminals.

I thought back to the crowds after the execution, rushing after the prison truck with Bin Laden's corpse on board and its windows sealed shut. Hordes of people pursued it as if they had gone mad.

The whole world had gone mad.

6

The very first time that I went to get the binoculars out of the bathroom, my daughter spotted me.

'What's that?' she asked.

'Nothing … It's medicine.'

'I know what it is. It's Hui Yuan Kidney Tonic,' she said triumphantly.

I couldn't believe it.

'How do you know that?'

'I saw it on TV. "Hui Yuan Kidney Tonic's a hot seller. Good for your man and good for you too!"'

She was very good at parroting the adverts. She mimicked the voices perfectly – it didn't matter what they were advertising. From 'Have you had a drink today? – Robust Company Foods' to 'Da Bao hair and skin products – for tomorrow and every day' and from 'Mei Yuan Chun wrinkle remover' right the way to 'An Er Le sanitary towels – fresh and cool and never leak'. We snickered behind our hands. Grown ups couldn't say things like that out loud, but it sounded hilarious when a kid said it. But this time I didn't know what to say. I wasn't up to explaining what a kidney tonic was, or how it could be 'good' for your man and for you too.

'You wouldn't understand,' I told her.

But she wasn't giving up.

'Why not?'

'Because these are grown-up things, not for kids,' I said. What did I mean? The binoculars were something kids shouldn't know about, a secret to be kept hidden.

'I do understand!' she yelled. 'I do! I do!'

She grabbed my bag. I held on to it. What if my wife heard her shrieking?

'I'll buy you a toy!'

'Now!'

'No, not right now.'

'I want it now!' she shouted.

'Why can't she have it straight away?' My wife had appeared out of nowhere. Had she seen anything?

'I'm busy,' I said.

'But aren't you on your way out?' she said. 'Don't worry, I'll bring her back up afterwards.'

There was no way out of it.

As they escorted me down the stairs we passed some of our neighbours.

'Where are you off to?' they asked my daughter.

'To buy a toy,' she said.

'Then you make sure get your daddy to buy you a nice one,' they teased. 'He can afford it.'

I hugged the bag tight. I couldn't let anyone find out what was inside it, no one at all. Especially not the neighbours.

It was like being kidnapped. By my daughter. She was a sweet kid, everyone said they loved her. Her mother and I used to joke 'If you walk out on me, just leave the girl.' Though recently that joke had gone a little sour.

A family with a daughter had a constant source of amusement. Laughter, tears, even a hissy fit was fun. When she asked difficult questions, you could just laugh them off. She was only three – who the fuck wanted to be serious?

At home she was so much fun it almost made you lazy. We were as childish as our kid. We bought her whatever she wanted. If she liked it, so did we.

Soon we were trawling around the department stores, picking and choosing, my daughter dragging me along like an idiot in her wake. I still had my arms wrapped round that bag with the binoculars. They seemed to have their infrared lenses fixed on me, driving me frantic. The assistant at the toy counter looked like he was on to me. He kept glancing at me and then at my daughter.

My daughter was holding a blue Pikachu kitty.

'How much is that?' asked my wife.

'Fifty yuan,' said the man, holding out five fingers.

Fifty yuan for a piece of old rubbish like that? My wife just reached in her purse. She hardly ever bargained. I'd always liked that about her, especially before we got married. I was going to earn the money, after all, and what's the point of earning it unless you spend it? But now I couldn't bear her buying it.

'No,' I said.

'I want it!' screamed my daughter.

'What about a discount?' asked my wife.

'That's already a discount,' said the assistant. 'This Pikachu kitty is a best seller.'

'We're not getting it!' I shouted.

'I want it!' screamed my daughter.

'Give it back!' I ordered.

My daughter started to make a run for it. I chased after her.

'No!' she shouted and hugged it to her chest, on the point of tears.

The assistant gave us a pitying look. He knew we'd have to buy it to cover up the emptiness of our lives.

'Can't you see how much she likes it?' he said. 'What price a child's happiness? I'm sure you do everything just for her, don't you.'

This was pure emotional blackmail.

'OK, let her have it,' said my wife. 'She really wants it.'

'No!' I said, grabbing for the toy.

My daughter ran off, shouting 'I want it!'

A crowd of people was staring at us, some of them familiar faces. Why was I behaving like this? I had more important matters to deal with. I still had those things it the bag, but instead of acting discreetly, I was making myself the centre of attention. But there was no way I was going to just stop and slink away.

'The money's nothing to you, is it, sir?' the assistant said. 'A big company boss like you, a very successful man ... '

'No I'm not!' I said.

'Then how can you afford to live in a posh area like this?' he said with a smile.

'I don't live here.'

He smiled again. It made my skin crawl. It was true. I was rich. Or rather, I had money enough for people to try and con me or blackmail me. I had money to bribe clients and splash it around, enough money to anaesthetise myself. Dammit, I had money but so what?

'Just buy it,' my wife said.

'I'm not giving in,' I yelled. 'I'd rather throw my money in the sea.' The whole shop was trying to get me to buy it now. 'Just mind your own business,' I shouted. 'Get off to your hellhole homes!'

I lashed out at one of the men in the front of the crowd, sending him reeling.

'What's wrong with you?' screeched my wife. 'You've been like this for a week. If you hate your wife and daughter so much, why don't you just tell us?'

She wasn't going to let me forget this. She was sick and tired of me, just as I was heartily sick of her. I smiled.

'Dad doesn't love us,' my daughter said. I couldn't believe it. My wife shot me a glance and tried to shush our daughter.

She had a guilty conscience too. But the kid went on. 'I know who Daddy loves.'

My wife went pale.

'Daddy's in love with someone else.'

'Quiet!' my wife yelled.

'It's true, it's true! Daddy's in love with someone else!'

I gave the child a slap and she burst into tears.

My wife took our daughter in her arms.

'Don't you dare hit her!'

I slapped the girl again. Blood trickled from her nose. There was no going back now.

'What way is that to treat a child?' shouted my wife, incandescent with rage. 'What does she know about anything? How could you? What kind of a father are you? What kind of a husband are you?'

What kind of a husband was I? I didn't visit prostitutes. I didn't keep a mistress. I'd provided well for both of them. I'd done more than enough.

7

I don't know how my daughter discovered my secret. She was only three years old but she could see right through me. Maybe it was my wife. She always had tabs on me. I must have let something slip when I was going out. Or perhaps I'd said something about the woman upstairs, something that made her quietly fix her eyes on me, and the kid had picked up on it. The thought of all that happening right in front of my nose – completely without my knowledge – made me shudder.

That flat opposite seemed to have been made for me. I couldn't imagine why it was still deserted. Our neighbourhood had the hottest properties in town, people usually snapped them up as soon as they went on the market. The window was easy to open, and I never met anyone hanging around. And it was bang opposite my own balcony. Maybe this flat was a trap, a trap set especially for me. Didn't I see someone standing at the window, right at the start? I went over there to investigate, started spying myself, and the result was that I became the person spied upon. I was getting paranoid.

I was convinced the woman had seen me and my wife arguing in the street, that she'd heard the noise, rushed to the balcony, looked down and seen me. I longed for her to ask what the trouble was. 'Problems in our sex life,' I would have said. But she never asked, even when I met her in the lift, even though there was no one else around. I was desolate.

I didn't dare go to the flat. The next day I didn't go to work. I couldn't stay still, I just wandered around, waiting for darkness. And then? Well, then I wanted to go to the flat so that I could see her. See her sitting up in bed, see how she sat up.

I called Water. I wanted to talk about women – I'd never done that before. But his mobile was switched off. He must have been hanging out with some whore, maybe fucking her right at that moment, for all I knew. I pictured the woman in my mind, the sordid scene. What a loser. I wandered down the street. The day dragged on and on, until darkness fell and the city glowed red.

Still no answer from Water.

I sneaked back into the building opposite. People stared at me in the lift, but I stared back. I didn't care if they saw me. I just needed to see with my own eyes how bleak her life was. The world was full of wretched people like her. She sat up in the darkness, but he ignored her, and he would ignore her no matter whether she sat up or not. He didn't care whether she sat up or lay down. Even if she sat up in bed all night, that husband of hers would never talk to her. He was dreaming about other women.

The darkness hid his infidelity.

But they weren't at home. Perhaps they were still out for a stroll. I waited. I waited a long time, but I was ready to wait all night long to share her loneliness. I was too tired to stand, so I crouched down and rested my chin on the windowsill. I didn't dare take my eyes off their window. They came back. I stood up. They were talking. Finally it was bedtime. They got into bed. The way she stood at the head of the bed in her nightie almost broke my heart. The light went out. They lay side by side. Through the binoculars, their bodies glowed. She hadn't taken her nightie off.

He took her in his arms.

Then he kissed her.

He began to caress her. She was lying with her eyes shut. He lay on his side, his movements slow and very gentle. Starting at the top and going down, he stroked every part of her, not missing an inch, like a real expert. Slowly, gradually, his hands reached down to her crotch. She trembled as his hands moved in, delicately, then accepted his touch and lay still, her eyes still shut. He just lay next to her, using his hands to bring her to a climax. Time passed slowly, freakishly slowly. Finally, she gave a shudder. She gripped his hand tight. Then she turned towards him and embraced him, panting, her head on his chest, bliss written on her face. But how could this be happening? I wanted to burst through their window and rescue her from all his lies.

But I couldn't.

She sat up in bed and reached for a box of tissues on the bedside table – luxury tissues, no doubt. She wiped herself and lay down again.

Silence.

So that was it. He had told her he couldn't get it up – that he was unwell, or tired, or impotent – but he wouldn't ignore her needs. 'I can satisfy you. I'll do it to you.' How completely considerate. How reasonable.

In Shanghai they've used the old slogan, Serve the People, for the marriage contract: wives promise to 'serve' their husbands regularly. And now he was serving her, wasn't he?

His service had been painstaking. It took him a long time too, lying on his side while his hands rubbed back and forth. She never took her nightie off. Sometimes I wondered if she'd fallen asleep, or maybe even he had. But then his arm would shift.

It was a long, slow chore for him. There was no way he would enjoy it, however beautiful the woman. He was Sisyphus pushing his rock up the hill, pushing without stopping for even a moment, otherwise all his effort would be wasted. Now and then he shifted and changed hands. He wouldn't give up, he wouldn't give her up. Serve the People.

Would he be sorry one day, sorry he'd let her know he could do this for her? That he'd made a rod for his own back?

I couldn't go home. I was like a stray dog. I stood at the

window, then crouched, then sat. The noise of a car faded into the distance. Maybe I drifted off to sleep, but I don't think so. A kind of sadness crept over me, as though that night I'd been robbed of everything. I smelled the bleak air of dawn, heard voices and footsteps, the clatter of pots and pans. She'd be busy in her kitchen, a contented housewife showing her gratitude, devoting herself to her husband.

But it was all a lie.

Later that day I bumped into her by the lift. As usual she was laden with bags – a plastic bag of groceries and another bag full of spring onions, garlic and greens. I studied her in the mirror. She looked just as contented as she had when she was resting on her husband's chest. If she only knew what a con it all was, what her husband was really like, how he was treating her – she'd be mortified. She might try to kill herself in shock and despair. I'd stop her, of course. After she found out the truth, she'd be helpless. Perhaps she might come and cry on my shoulder. God, was that it? Had I been after her from the start? It had never occurred to me it might all be because of her, that he masturbated because she didn't want to have sex with him.

No. She had absolutely no idea. It was as if she was still wearing her nightie. As if I could see her body under it. Stark naked. A stranger's body. I'd never seen a stranger's naked body. It was holding a bag of spring onions, garlic and greens.

'Have you been shopping?' I stammered.

'Yes,' she answered.

A large river eel squirmed in the plastic bag.

'Are you going to have eel for dinner?'

'Yes.'

There was an awkward pause. Somewhere a pile-driver

66

was at work, the sound close by, yet somehow still remote.

'A balanced diet must be very important for both of you.'

She smiled.

'Life has got better,' she said.

Thump. Thump. Thump.

'Does nutrition really make a difference?'

'Having something to eat always makes a difference.'

'But you still can't plug a leak,' I said.

Another smile. She shifted the bag of greens to her other hand, the stalks nodding as the bags knocked against each other.

The door opened and a crowd of people jostled into the lift.

How I hated her.

I rushed over to the empty flat. She was killing the eel. She was covering it with wine in a stainless steel pot, bottle in one hand, lid in the other, pouring in the wine then slamming down the lid. The pot shuddered as she wiped a few splashes of wine from her face, so she picked up the thick wooden chopping board and placed it on top. She started to clear up the worktop, but the eel shoved the lid off the pot and started wriggling out. She shrieked and tried to push it back in again as it tumbled on to the floor. She yelled and grabbed at it and her husband came running in from the sitting room. They tried to corner it, but it slipped out of their grasp, slithering unhurriedly, deliberately, powerfully, as if completely unafraid. It reared up and looked straight at them and she shrieked again and tried to make a joke of it, jumping up and down as if she had an itch. But then fear overwhelmed her and she grabbed her husband and hid behind him, screaming with terror.

I always told my customers to make up medicines in an

earthenware pot – not that it makes any difference, to be honest, but it was all part of the ritual. So when I saw her one day carrying a bag with an earthenware pot, I knew straight away what she was up to. I even recognised some of the ingredients for the tonic she was making: desert broomrape, five-flavours, snake's bed, wolfberry kernels.

That evening I heard a woman calling for her on the stairs. There was a mutter of some mysterious conversation, but as the woman was leaving I caught her final words.

'Remember, whatever you do, don't wash it,' she said. 'Just put it in as it is.'

Whatever were they talking about?

I went straight back to the flat opposite. She was in the kitchen, with the herbs on the counter next to the earthenware pot. She opened up a bag, took out a round, purple lump and put it into the pot. It must have been sticky, because afterwards she gave her hands a good scrub in the sink. Then she carefully put in the herbs and some water, working slowly, intently, like some kind of ritual. She brought it to a fierce boil and then turned it down to simmer, watching it closely all the time.

Something was wrong. She grabbed for the pot, burning her hands, then reached for a cloth and picked it up. There must have been a crack. She tipped it all into another pot, turned over the earthenware pot to look at the base, dropped it into the rubbish bin and ran out of the flat. I ran downstairs as well, and saw her dart into a grocery to buy another pot. But she came straight out again. She tried another, but no luck. The shops were shutting – it was nine o'clock – so she ran to the street and called a cab. Why did she need an earthenware pot so badly? She was beside herself. I got in a cab and told the driver to follow her. He gave me a pointed smile.

'It's not what you think,' I said. 'If she kills herself, it'll be your fault.'

I don't know why I said it, but it was enough to wipe the grin off the driver's face. He raced after her until the cab in front stopped by a long flight of stairs. She leaped out and ran up the steps to a Japanese shop. It was closed, so she started hammering on the door. After a while an angry woman called out from inside.

'What's the matter?'

'I need an earthenware pot.'

'What do you want a pot for at this time of night?'

'I'm boiling medicine.'

The door opened a crack, letting a shaft of light out.

'You're off your head,' said the shopkeeper, opening the door a crack. A shaft of light spilled out on to the steps.

'Thank you. Thank you so much.'

'What's so urgent about the medicine?'

'It's a tonic.'

'A tonic? What kind of a tonic?'

'It's a secret recipe … '

'A secret recipe?' The shopkeeper wasn't angry any more, she was intrigued. I pictured her holding the pot to her chest, as if to say, I'll only give it to you if you tell me about the recipe.

'A kidney tonic,' my neighbour muttered.

She came back down the steps, cradling the pot in her arms, and looked for a taxi. She stood there in the darkness on the windswept street. Maybe I could pretend I just happened to be passing by. We could share a cab back home – a shame I hadn't brought the car – or we could just stand there in the wind and the dark. But she would insist on getting home. She was brewing up a kidney tonic. She clasped the pot in her arms as if it was a baby. She didn't have a baby, would never have one. It was as if she was holding her husband, or rather, her own life.

Where were the vagrants, the gangsters that prowl the streets? Would one of them accost her as she stood there in the dark?

That night I had a dream. She was in her kitchen making up the tonic. Her husband was out and the door to their flat was ajar. I burst in and embraced her from behind. I knocked the pot on to the floor with my elbow and it smashed to smithereens. All the mixture poured out. She reached for the pot but I gripped her tight. She started to struggle. 'Damn it, why are you making kidney tonic soup?' I shouted. 'Don't you know how your husband has weakened his kidneys? Don't you know? When you're getting your thrills, he's thinking of another woman! And you're still faithful to him? Why? You stupid, useless woman!' She shook like wheat in a winnowing machine, her mouth wide open, gasping for air. But I showed her no mercy, I just kept shouting, on and on. She collapsed to her knees and I sat astride her, as if she was a mare. I grabbed at her nightie and yanked it up to her neck. She was naked, the nightie hanging forwards across her face like a dog wearing a cone. I whipped her and she writhed in pain. There was tonic all over the floor, there was no saving it now. I was hurting her, she was hurting me, whipping me with the cloth in her hand … I came.

Then one day, she wasn't there.

8

I longed to see her, but she had disappeared. Her husband was alone in the flat – nervous, uneasy. Did he have some idea where she had gone? He slept alone that night. He didn't sprawl all over the bed, he rolled her quilt up into tube and stretched out beside it. Then he wanked himself off on to the quilt.

Every evening he went out for a stroll, on his own. He always went for his walk, even when there was a storm. He took out his umbrella and held it out, as if she was walking along beside him. I was stuck at home watching TV, channel hopping. I'd just caught a glimpse of him from the balcony when I heard the news reader say there had been some progress in the kidney theft case.

'After the arrest of a nurse and the housewife who bought the kidney, a third suspect has been detained in connection with this case ...'

Three portraits flashed up on screen, the faces pixellated to protect the suspects' identities. But I could tell it was her.

Her husband was walking around outside in the pouring rain, holding out the umbrella, one shoulder soaked right through.

A day or so afterwards, the flat upstairs exploded into banging and clattering. I ran up to find the police turning the whole place upside down. There was herbal medicine all over the floor. They eyed me suspiciously and wouldn't let me in, but I stood my ground. And who should be standing right by the door looking bemused but her husband. The man who did that thing. The man I'd seen doing that thing. He was almost close enough for me to touch. It was unreal. He glanced at me, then looked down again. He must have thought I knew why the police were there. Did he know I knew all their little secrets too? He was completely crushed. She had trusted this guy and he had betrayed her. I could have wept for her.

When the police left I asked him if there was anything we could do. He just said 'No.'

'So you're going to leave your wife in prison for ever?' My heart skipped at the words 'your wife'. Then I flared up. 'She did so much for you and now you're going to see her rot for life?'

'I can't do a thing about it,' he said. 'I've pulled all the strings I can, but it's no use…'

'Maybe I can do something,' I said.

He looked up at me.

'Do you know where this kidney came from?' I asked.

'She didn't say. They never said either. A nurse got it, my wife's friend. She said the hospital was just throwing it away.'

The nurse … that elegant woman who always kept her hand in her pocket?

'How could she do such a thing?' He was angry now. 'It was perfectly obvious it would be discovered before she'd got her money. That nurse was crazy. We're powerless. People with power do these things and people without don't, but she did it anyway. She must have been crazy. And my wife must have been crazy too. She never said a word about what it was. I just thought it tasted strange. It made me feel a bit sick, but she said it was a wonderful tonic … '

How could she have believed such rubbish?

I thought back to the woman's words: 'Remember, whatever you do, don't wash it. Just put it in as it is … '

'That tonic was made with Bin Laden's kidney,' I said, fixing him with a hard look.

'Impossible!' he cried.

'Just because you didn't know about it doesn't mean it isn't true.' I couldn't be sure it was Bin Laden's kidney, but I knew what I had to do to save her.

'Are you really sure it was his?' he asked, faintly.

'It was!'

He threw up all over the floor.

'That Chinese-American was a bastard too!' he shouted. 'He must have reported her. He'd come here specially to get himself a new kidney. He was already in hospital, waiting for the operation.' He grabbed my hand. 'Please help me. Please, please, I beg you … You're my only hope.'

There he was, begging like a dog. The man who did that thing. Her husband. The man she'd done everything for. The man she'd trusted. I wanted to weep for her. I wanted to kick him away.

'Why should I help you? Why should I? Why?'

9

The only way I could save her was blackmail. Someone must have had their eye on Bin Laden's kidney for a long time. He had to be killed, and killed in the name of the law – there was no way the hospital could have removed it unless the court was involved. They probably even sentenced him to death so someone could get hold of his kidney. But the courts wouldn't have dared to do anything without a nod from those in charge. This was a society that killed people for personal gain. Obviously the courts would insist they'd handed down a sentence according to the law, the hospital would protest that it wasn't Bin Laden's kidney after all. But with the evidence I got from Water, no one would believe them. Those in power would be afraid that they'd all be dragged into the ensuing scandal. They'd come down on me like a ton of bricks, of course. And my old friend Water, the man who'd helped me sell those Hami melons all those years ago, would get in trouble too. I was confronting the entire regime. But I didn't care about myself. All I wanted was to save her. Nothing more.

I did what I had to do.

I went into the detention centre on my own. I told her husband to wait outside, said they would only let me in if I was alone. I don't know if he believed me. He had no choice. I was the only one who could save her. I'd be in there myself soon enough, paying the price. There's no way the people I had threatened would let me off. It would be my turn next.

And I'd bring down a lot of people with me. The trial would follow its inevitable logic to the end.

The warden was clearly astonished at the size of the bribe I slipped into his palm and led me in with great courtesy. She was much thinner, so thin that it almost felt like a crime for me to be well-covered. I said her husband had left, told her he had something to do, and asked the warden to lead us out a different way.

'I'll give you a ride,' I said.

I hoodwinked her.

She got into my car.

She had never been in my car before. It was strange, unreal. I backed out of the prison car park with her looking behind, guiding me in a low voice. I had never heard her speak so quietly. I was uncomfortable, confused, as if I was a thief and she was the swag. Or rather, as if she was my prey. At last I could speak to her. I had waited so long. Everything was prepared. There was no time for hesitation, even if it hurt her, even if it killed her. She was still looking behind the car, with no idea what all this was about. A curious sense of satisfaction stole over me, testament to the streak of cruelty I had discovered in myself many years ago.

It was after the Tiananmen incident – I was still a student. Soldiers chased me into a blind alley, with nowhere to hide. I knocked on every door in the alley, but no one would take me in. So I hid in a doorway, shrinking back into it as far as I could. Army boots trampled past like stampeding horses. I was squeezing myself in to the point of collapse. I was terrified. I didn't know if I was dead or alive. The only way I could tell was to pinch my thighs and see if it hurt. I pinched so hard the pain was excruciating. All I could feel was pain, and the harder I pinched the less I was afraid. That was when I started to enjoy pinching. I pinched my first girlfriend almost to death. I used to pinch my wife until she shrieked with pain. Now I pinch my daughter.

I put my foot down and the car shot forward. She gripped on to the sides of the seat.

'Are you afraid?' I asked.

She smiled and shook her head.

'Doesn't your husband ever drive like this?'

She shook her head again. She knew absolutely nothing. Sometimes I hated her for being so ignorant.

'It sounds like the kidney didn't help,' I said.

She flushed scarlet and turned to look out of the window. A flock of seagulls circled above us as we reached the new bridge, symbol of our city's modernisation. It's one of the world's longest suspension bridges, so they say. You can still just about make out the slogan from when it was opened on the steel hawsers: 'Taking a leap into the world.' It was like she was seeing the slogan for the first time.

'Do you know why your husband has kidney deficiency?'

She grabbed for the door handle.

'Stop the car,' she said. 'I've forgotten something.'

'Where.'

'Back there,' she said.

I smiled. What could she have possibly left there? Was she just avoiding the truth? Could she have known what her husband was getting up to all along? A dreadful thought. No. It was impossible. No woman could bear it. All the same I felt flustered.

'Forget it,' I said.

'But it's important.'

'Important, huh?' I said. 'Your husband's important, but look at what kind of man he is.'

'Let me out,' she insisted.

'Do you know what kind of man your husband is? Do you know what he gets up to behind your back?'

'I want to get out!' she shouted.

'Do you know or don't you?' I yelled back. I was going to tell her everything. It was my last chance. 'Every morning when you're busy getting breakfast ready, he's in there, he's ... wanking.'

It was a struggle to get the words out, but what a relief.

'I want to get out!'

I reached out and held her in a fierce grip, but she kept struggling, pulling at the door handle again and again. She was slippery as an eel.

'I saw it, I saw everything! And you still ... you still actually ... ' The steering wheel twitched in my hand. A lorry loaded with sand veered into the oncoming lane, screeching and zigzagging wildly across the road.

'Let me tell you a story,' she said.

When I got home the house was quiet. My daughter was having her afternoon nap. My wife was taking a shower. She came out into the afternoon sunlight, wrapped in a towel. I refused to get excited about her any more. From now on, I would ignore the rustle of clothes as she took them off and dropped them to the floor to get into her nightie.

'Have you had dinner?'

'No.'

'I'll make something for you.'

I turned on the TV and flicked through the channels. Nothing on the news about the kidney. I wasn't out of the

woods yet, but there was plenty of other crime to look into
– fake goods, illegal trading, tax evasion … And even if
they did investigate me, even if they did find my dodgy
supplements had killed a few people, well, I had only done
it for my family, to give them a better standard of living.
They couldn't prove anything.

10

Let me tell you a story.

*A long, long time ago, there was a husband who used to
masturbate when his wife was not looking. But she knew all
about it.*

*At first she had absolutely no idea what to do. It was quite
some time since they had enjoyed sexual relations – he said he
couldn't get it up. Perhaps it was the pressure of work. He was
running a big business, after all, and she understood how hard
that was. She was happy with her life, though because of her
husband's impotence they had no children. But in the end she
lost the courage to go on living in this way. Had he fallen in
love with someone else? She couldn't imagine who it might be,
but she worried the woman could appear at any moment and
her husband would demand a separation. The same thought
had occurred to her many times, but the idea he might suggest
it himself terrified her. Were there any good men in this world?*

*One day the wife went to the herbalist and bought her husband
a packet of Hui Yuan kidney tonic. Everybody knew about Hui*

Kidney Tonic

Yuan kidney tonic, it was advertised on every street corner. Even children recited the jingles off by heart. She did not believe in fairy tales like that, of course, but she hoped it might give her husband a gentle reminder. It should be perfectly obvious why she was giving it to someone who basically had no sex life at all, but if he protested, if he refused to take the hint, she could always relent and say it was a tonic to build up his general health.

Her husband did not object, he just took his medicine and never said a word. Neither did he give up his secret pastime.

Gradually she became aware that her husband never went out in the evenings. He came home from work, ate dinner with her and stayed home all night. If he was forced to take a client out to dinner he would propose a few of the usual toasts and then find some pretext to leave – he certainly was an accomplished liar. There were times when she urged him to go out, but he just said 'You have no idea how tiresome these occasions are.' As soon as he returned to their flat he turned off his mobile , and if anyone called on their home number he would go to any lengths to avoid taking the call. The wife did not know if any of these calls were from a woman, but she did once take one that struck her as odd: when the caller heard her voice, he or she simply said nothing. Her husband told her to hang up. He said he could not think why anyone would make silent telephone calls. But then he refused to take any calls at all. He asked her to answer the telephone for him and say he had gone out.

He never spoke of a separation.

Sexual issues aside, their married life went on as normal. They began to take evening walks. Day after day, whatever the weather he would talk to his wife intimately about this and that. This special time they spent as a married couple made her happy. And every night he insisted on taking her into his arms before they went to sleep.

But one night, while her husband was holding her close, he said he wanted to bring her to orgasm.

At first she refused.

He explained he wanted to do it with his hand.

She still refused.

Since sexual relations were now impossible, he said, his impotence would become unbearable unless he could find a way to give his wife satisfaction. At the very mention of the word 'impotence' his face fell. Was his sorrow genuine, she wondered? And if so, was it because he really was impotent, or because he was unable to have intimate relations with someone else who might help him to perform? But she was afraid he would become suspicious if she questioned him.

She pleaded with him, saying that she did not want to in case he tired himself out. He seemed to be using his impotence as a form of blackmail.

In the end, she decided to let him have his way.

Do you have any idea what it feels like for a woman? A little dark, a little cold, a little sad. It feels as if you are looking on from a great distance. You are acutely aware of how everything gradually builds to a climax. The pleasure it gives is more direct than normal sexual intercourse, admittedly, but it is a short cut to a pleasure that is ice cold, compressed like a computer chip.

The wife told her husband it was a kind of rape. She said she felt like a prostitute, or rather, as if she was at an orgy with someone she knew cared nothing for her.

He adopted a new position every time. She remembered reading in a magazine that there were so many different positions you could try a new one every day of the year and still have *more to try.*

One day she understood this unconventional arrangement was keeping their relationship going. She couldn't help smiling to herself. If there was another sexual partner there would be no need for him to continue pleasuring himself, and he wouldn't keep pleasuring his wife unless he loved her. Her only regret was they would never have children.

Her husband's health became a constant worry. She had no idea what she would do without him – a sure sign of her love – so she decided to start preparing him tonics. At his age he ought to be taking supplements of all kinds. Whenever she heard about a good one, his wife would go out and buy it. As soon as a new product came on to the market, she had to have it. All her heart and soul were devoted to finding and preparing her husband tonics. She had never put much faith in any of them before, but now she understood why these concoctions commanded such a high price. It was almost as if a drug would be useless if it was too easy to buy.

'Give me your most expensive preparations,' she would say. 'I don't care how much it costs. I have money!'

In the end, she bought her husband a kidney.

Are you sure about this?
You can shut the book now.
Do you choose to read on?

The Hint

1

I had just lost my job. Again. I don't know why I kept losing jobs, I could never figure it out. I worked hard, I did whatever I was asked. I was a solid, reliable office toiler. One time the boss asked me to clean the sliding doors. I rubbed and rubbed until I thought I'd done a good job, but as soon as the boss stepped up to the door and it opened, a smear appeared on the glass and I lost my job. That time they told me to clean the door again, so I rubbed and rubbed the glass, and rubbed some more. When I stepped up to it to check, the door whooshed open, the glass all bright and shiny. But I lost the job anyway.

'It's not that you're no good,' said the boss.

It wasn't that I was no good, and it had nothing to do with the whole door incident. It's just that the world was one big lottery and it was completely random whether you won or lost – or so it seemed to me.

That day I went home, put my head down and slept. I slept right through until the next morning. I slept until I was woken by a banging on the bedroom door. It was my mum. I still lived with my parents, or rather, in their house, worst luck.

As soon as they realised I was still in bed and had lost my job they panicked.

'Get out of bed! Get out of bed!' shouted my dad, like he was worried I had died in the night or something. As if getting up would help me find another job. The chances of winning the lottery keep on going down, but the less hope there is of taking the jackpot the keener people are to win it.

'You're almost 30, whatever are you going to do?' my parents cried.

I was really only 25. This was all a fuss about nothing.

'OK, OK, I'll go and rob a bank.'

That shut them up. They were law-abiding people, respectable workers all their lives. When I did politics at school, they told us the proletariat was the heroic working class, but my parents weren't like that. Their kind of proletariat didn't own anything but they were so law-abiding they would never go and steal even if they were starving – real thieves are never actually short of food. That was the way my parents brought me up. I was never bad – the worst I ever did was watch bad people doing bad things and have a good laugh. So everybody pitied me at school. When we left, everybody took photos of all their friends, and wrote them cards and invited them to parties. But no one came near me.

I yawned, scratched my crotch and crawled out of bed.

Then the gang from middle school turned up.

They roared up on motorbikes, wearing army fatigues and revving their engines. Our elderly neighbours clasped their hands to their chests in terror – we didn't see many motorbikes round where I lived. The riders didn't care, just took off their helmets and tossed back their hair. After we graduated, everyone got themselves a high-flying job – everyone except me, that is. I carried on living in the run-down area where I'd always lived. Maybe I wasn't smart enough, but how had the rest of them got so smart? They all had motorbikes. If you gave me one for free, I couldn't even pay for a number plate.

'We'd starve if we only had our wages to live on,' they used to scoff.

Anyway, they'd come to invite me to a reunion dinner – a chance for the successful ones to show off to the ones who weren't successful.

'I'm too busy … ' I said. I stopped myself before I could add: 'I've got to go to work.'

'Just tell us when we can pick you up and we'll go together,' they said.

'Why am I such a big deal all of a sudden?'

'It's not because of you, it's her.'

She used to sit at the table in front of me in class and turn around to borrow my rubber. She was nothing much to look at, very skinny, but her arms were long and white and every time she borrowed my rubber, her arm bent at the elbow like it was a clamp. I started longing for that clamp – I wanted to put my rubber somewhere within its reach. Eventually I bought a special rubber with a nice smell. I thought she'd like it. But then one day the teacher spotted us and called the pair of us up to the front – the whole class burst out laughing.

The gang told me she was going to marry a wealthy man and my heart gave a thump.

'He drives a Lexus. Apparently, he's in real estate,' someone said.

'No, he's into futures,' someone else said.

'No, no. You're all wrong. He works in a subsidiary of the China Poly group.'

They all started arguing. They were all playing detectives, snooping into other people's wealth. He was certainly rich, they could agree that much, but nobody really knew how – a fact which only made him seem all the richer. He had mysteriously become rich the way I mysteriously kept losing my job.

I didn't know anything about it myself. I hadn't seen her for ages.

'So the bitch finally dropped you,' one said. 'She never even talked to you about marriage?'

I never imagined she would. She wasn't my girl.

She was the class beauty.

They all started wondering if he'd given her one back then, which got everyone reminiscing about taking girls to the cinema, getting to first base, swearing eternal love … they'd all had girlfriends. I was gutted. There really was nothing between her and me except for borrowing rubbers. But the way they were talking made me think there had been something momentous, some grand passion between us, and that she'd dumped me. I wanted to go find her, give her a slap and ask if she'd dumped me because I wasn't as smart as her fiancé. Because I didn't have a Lexus. But the more I wanted to ask her, the less I wanted to go to the dinner.

And when I found out Lexus would be there, there was no way I was going.

'Hey, stop being such an idiot,' they said. 'We'll stick up for you. We'll make a fool of that Lexus.'

Bikers jealous of a man on four wheels? I still wasn't going.

'Surely you're not afraid of him,' they said.

'Afraid? Me? You must be kidding!' I protested. Shit. What the hell was there to be afraid of anyway? There was never anything going on, not even a hint of a love affair, so why the hell would I be worried about being run down by a Lexus?

'OK, I'll go.'

2

She had become beautiful. And I mean truly lovely. As lovely as a brightly-painted lantern. And that lantern was hanging right in front of my eyes, dazzling me. Lexus was standing behind her. He was powerfully built, but unfortunately he was almost a midget. No amount of money would change that. This stocky little man jingled the car keys in his hand, damn it, like they were marbles.

'Is he really tall enough to drive a car?' someone asked.

'Can he reach the clutch?'

'Of course he can! He can put a pad under his feet, just like the boy hero Lei Feng!' There was a shout of laughter.

But he didn't seem to hear any of that. She was raising her arm – the same long, white arm I remembered – beckoning for everyone to come over for a photo, like some damn class monitor. None of us wanted to be in the picture. In fact, everyone insisted it should be just the two of them, pushing them together so they were shoulder to shoulder, putting their arms around each other's waists, making them stand cheek to cheek – 'To make it more intimate.'

But, guess what? To our surprise, Lexus objected.

'You don't need to get close in public if you're sleeping together,' he said. 'You only do it in public if you're not doing it in private.'

That shut everybody up. We all stood there, blinking in surprise. He went upstairs. She stamped her foot and ran after him. We didn't dare stare. So that's what it was like to be rich – you could do whatever the fuck you wanted. In the end we all got up to get him a drink. But no one wanted to go upstairs after them. They all said I should go first. I said no, so they started trying to push me up the stairs. I pushed back with all my might. Then who should turn up but Lexus, glass in hand.

'Hey, stop bullying the poor man,' he said.

'Poor man?' Everyone roared with laughter.

I glared round at them, but they took no notice and carried on laughing. He must have known. I definitely shouldn't have come. It was all very well for the rest of them, but I'd fallen right into a trap. Then he burst out laughing too. He laughed just like a frog, clasping fat arms to his chest. I started to relax.

The rest of them were still joking: 'Trust an honest man to get one over on you.'

'You mean him?' he asked, poking me with his finger, as if he was that paragon of official virtue, Judge Bao. More laughter. He stopped laughing and topped up my drink. 'I have ways of telling if you're a thief,' he said, raising his glass towards me and emptying it.

The others all chanted: 'Drink! Drink! Down it in one!'

So I did. I had to.

'Good,' said Lexus. 'People who drink and thieve are generally thieves, people who are honest and drink are generally honest. So he's not a thief.'

Everyone burst out laughing again. But Lexus wasn't laughing. He just opened another bottle and sat down beside me, ignoring the racket going on around us.

'Come on, let's drink,' he said and poured some more for both of us.

She nibbled seeds and looked bored, her face somehow pinched. He was deliberately ignoring her. Suddenly she stood up and tried to grab the glass out of his hand.

'If you get drunk, how are you going to get home?' she said.

'What are you worried about? Hitting a telegraph pole and dying is no big deal.'

There was a cheer at that. A real cheer. But she went red, then white, and looked like she was going to cry.

'I don't care about you dying, I care about the car.'

'The car?' he said. 'It cost less than a hundred thousand. Peanuts.'

'Wow!' everyone said. 'That's money talking.'

'Where the hell did you get so much money from?' someone asked.

'I robbed a bank,' he said.

That stunned everybody. Then they started grinning.

'Have you ever seen someone with a wallet walking down the street? Reach out and it's yours,' he said. 'Have you ever seen jewels on display in a shop window? Get a knife and a bag and grab them, and they're all yours. Aren't they?'

A roar of laughter.

3

If he'd talked seriously about business, he'd have got himself throttled. As it was, everyone thought he was great. Even me. At the end of the evening, I got him to drive me home. Three days later, he turned up at my house in the Lexus. He stood there jingling his keys as the neighbours gawped, then came in and plonked himself down. My house was so ramshackle it practically needed propping up, and the floor was uneven, but he just sat right down on it and said: 'Let's have a drink.'

I couldn't imagine why. He pulled out a bottle of *baijiu* and some nibbles – duck legs, duck wings, shredded squid and a packet of dipping sauce. I couldn't believe he had all this stuff in his pockets when he was driving here in the Lexus. I laughed and drank up.

'I had to sneak out,' he said, taking a gulp. 'I nearly didn't make it.' He sneaked a glance through one of the cracks – my door was full of cracks. It dawned on me that she wasn't here and that, without her, something was missing. Still, she gave us something in common. Maybe I could tell him how I felt.

'She's on my case day in day out,' he said, 'going on about this and that, telling me drinking's not good for you, that alcohol poisons the system and hardens the liver.' She sounded like a model citizen. I'd never seen that in her at middle school. Maybe women are always women, and automatically turn into model citizens like they can automatically breastfeed when they have babies.

'That's just how she is,' I said.

'It's so annoying,' he said.

Why couldn't she lecture me instead? I stood up.

'You're all right,' I snapped. 'She loves you.'

'That's true,' he said. 'When she wants me, she slips both arms under my armpits, and clamps her hands on my shoulder blades.'

I stared at him and laughed.

'Where did you get your money?' I asked.

'Money? Huh! It's all stolen,' he said. I laughed again. 'Really,' he continued. 'You don't believe me? Well, you do what you do in this business – sometimes you use all the tricks of the trade and sometimes you don't. Like when you're starting something new, just put a toe in the water. If you do that the right way then you're half way there. Put it in wrong and you'll be sorry.'

What a big head. So this was why he wanted to spend the evening drinking with me. Some people have to boast all the time. They just love showing off how clever they are, making other people look dumb. They love giving you a shock. He wasn't even looking at me. He was just listening to the sound of his own voice.

'It's not worth trying to get money out of old folks, nor your average housewife either, they only have enough to do the shopping. As for young girls, they're jail bait. If you touch them and you slip up, you get arrested. You're better off nicking a housewife's purse and getting yourself a hooker ... '

I burst out laughing. It sounded like he'd given this some serious thought.

'Banks, that's where the money is,' he went on.

'Banks?' I blurted out. 'But they're like Fort Knox.'

He looked at me sideways.

'You don't understand a thing, do you? Sure, security's tight but that doesn't matter. The cashiers are shut away behind reinforced glass, sure, and the trays are so small you have to scrabble around for the cash, but there's always a way. Each little safe is packed tight with bank notes, packed tight as pancakes. Get it?'

He slapped me on the back. I jumped. I was day-dreaming like an idiot. I pulled myself together and jabbed my finger at him.

'You're going to rob a bank. That's what you're saying, isn't it.'

He leaped to his feet and rushed to the door, straining to hear if there was anyone outside. He looked like a criminal on the run. Maybe I'd gone too far. He gripped the bottle in his hand so hard it looked like it was going to break.

'Are you going to turn me in?' he demanded.

'Why would I do that?' I said. 'You're hardly going to rob my house, there's nothing here. And I'd get nothing as a reward.' I carried on trying to humiliate myself, trying to make myself look dumb. I wanted to lay my heart bare. I wanted to shout 'I'm no good! I haven't even got a girlfriend. Why would she ever go for someone like me instead of you?'

Eventually he sat down again. He looked at me for a long time.

'There'll be a job in two days' time,' he said.

4

I started listening to the news. I'd never paid any attention before, certainly not the local news. But there I was, jumping to my feet every time they played the title sequence. I didn't dare watch at home, or anywhere I might be recognised. I ran all the way to a shop a few streets away and sneaked into the middle of a crowd of migrant workers who used to peer at a black and white TV in the window.

I was waiting for news of a bank robbery.

But there was nothing. Nothing for days on end.

How stupid. What an arsehole. Why did I ever believe a man like that?

But a week later, the bastard turned up again. Still driving the Lexus, still jingling the keys. This time, he brought her along. I was so embarrassed when I saw her. I thought he'd brought her along to see what an arsehole I was. They must have been having a good laugh about me.

I gave her a wary smile, but she didn't smile back.

'Were you two doing business the other day?'

'What?' I yelped. 'Business?'

He gave me a wink.

'Yeah … sure,' I said. I don't know why I lied for him. It was as if I was mesmerised by his wink.

He exploded in giggles, as if someone had jabbed him in the ribs.

'You're trying to fool me too,' she said. 'You're ganging up on me.'

I started laughing too.

'No more deals!' She was almost hysterical. 'And don't leave me behind!'

'So where's the money going to come from if I don't do deals?' he said, all serious now. But all I could think of was the way he had talked about stealing. I laughed even harder. 'If we don't have money, what are you going to eat, or wear? What about the car, damn it, or the wedding?' The more he talked, the more he got worked up. Something had really got to him – he was losing it. I reached out and tried to calm him down, but it just seemed to wind him up even more. 'What do you women know about anything?' he shouted. 'All you do is eat, get dressed and spend money. I'd give anything to be a woman and get taken around all day every day and have nothing to worry about. Did I ask to be a man? Did I?'

He flung the door open and stormed out. I followed, my heart in my mouth. I thought he was going to kill himself, I don't know why. I caught up with him and grabbed his arm. He tried to pull away but I hung on. We weren't just two guys after the same girl any more, it was like we were fellow sufferers.

'Life's such a bitch,' he said. 'It always ends up like this. Always.'

'I know, I know.' I nodded. 'And it's men who get the raw deal. We never asked to be a man.' It was like I was going to kill myself.

'You have no idea ... I was putting together a huge deal last week and she screwed it all up.'

I jumped. Did he mean that bank job?

93

Just then she came out of the house. I was suddenly furious, as if she'd screwed up my deal, not his. They got into the car and he started the engine. I stuck my head through the window.

'So … what's going to happen about that business?'

He looked up.

'It'll have to wait until next week.'

She was giving me a strange look. I ignored it. I stood up straight and gave his shoulder a squeeze.

'You be careful,' I said.

5

They robbed a savings bank. They forced open the iron door to the cashiers' counter and smashed up the security camera. It was chaos. How fucking audacious was that? The chairs were all tipped over, there was paper all over the floor and scuff marks as if they'd dragged out something heavy. Everyone in the crowd outside the shop window was riveted to the TV, standing there completely silent as the newsreader declared: 'The Qiao Xi branch of the Construction Bank has achieved notable success in raising alertness and strengthened security measures have been put in place.'

That sounded pretty fishy.

I ran down to the bank. It was open for business as normal, the staff sitting calmly behind the counter. There were no customers, not a single scrap of paper on the floor. It was all spick and span. Unnaturally so, in fact. It looked like someone had just given it a coat of paint. Of course. On TV it was only good news, never bad news. So if something was reported as extremely good news, in reality things were pretty bad, and if they reported anything bad at all, it had to mean there had been a total disaster. They had a wonderful way of putting a positive spin on bad news: after a flood they'd report on disaster relief and flood prevention, after a bank robbery they'd report on tightening security … I smiled. Everybody loved watching a good disaster, their eyes glued to the TV. They'd stand on tired feet outside the shop, nowhere to sit down, slapping at the mosquitoes, watching something that could never happen that had actually happened. A bank job. How fucking audacious was that! They'd gasp in astonishment at the fistfuls of recovered bank notes the police displayed to the cameras, cursing and swearing because they couldn't have any of it themselves. They'd rail at theft and robbery, bribery and corruption precisely because they weren't thieving and taking bribes themselves. They'd picture themselves in the robbers' shoes and get really pissed off.

The next time I saw him he was driving a Merc. I couldn't imagine why he'd given up the Lexus. Maybe he needed the Merc for business. Why shouldn't he, if he had the cash? But if I was him I'd have been a bit more careful with my money. He said he'd take me for a spin. As soon as I was in, he put his foot down and the Merc took off like a racehorse. I gripped the window frame, hanging on for dear life.

I'm a timid man. I hate speed. When I was at middle school, there was a class where we all had to talk about our dreams for the future. The other kids talked about being football stars, film stars, pop stars. They bragged about becoming business magnates. In their minds, they were flying high. When it came to me, I couldn't get a word out. The whole class burst out laughing, even her. She clearly thought I was an idiot. To her, I was an ugly duckling who'd never be able to fly. In those days no one had time for stupidity, you only opened your mouth to boast, you only talked about flying high. So everyone was boasting, everyone was flying high. Everyone was part of lightning-speed development.

He was flying at top speed now and humming a little tune. I was flying too and realising that when you were really flying you couldn't feel yourself flying at all, damn it. The difference between a good car and a bad car was whether it could fly. The difference between a good guy and a stupid one was whether you could get her to fly with you. Finally I'd understood. Too bad it was too late.

'How is she?'

'She's fine,' he said. 'We've got the Merc now, so of course she's fine.'

'Does she get scared when you go this fast?'

'Scared? ...Well, she slips both arms under mine, and clamps her hands back on to my shoulders.'

He roared with laughter. I laughed along. We both laughed loudly.

When he dropped me off I asked him when he was planning his next job.

'What?'

'Damn it, don't play dumb with me!' I thumped him.

He chuckled. 'Maybe on National Day.'

'National Day!' I yelped. 'It's the 50th anniversary. There'll be troops all over the place.'

'So?'

'There'll be cops everywhere … '

'I know.' He smiled. 'I also know that the tightest security will be at the Commercial Bank on East Chang'An Avenue.'

6

I went straight to East Chang'An Avenue.

The Commercial Bank was jam-packed. The customers were making deposits and withdrawals, smacking bulging envelopes full of bank notes against their palms as they went in. Of course, this was bonus season. If I'd got a job, I'd have got a holiday bonus too. It could have been me going into the bank rustling fistfuls of bank notes.

A tall, thin man stuck a pile of notes into his briefcase and went out. A guy started following him – someone I knew. I smiled at him as he went past, but he pretended not to see me. The tall man got on a motorbike. The guy did too, a Honda 250 which he'd left there before. He was going to jump him in some back street. Or no. He wouldn't get off the bike, or jump the man himself: he'd have an accomplice. The accomplice would be riding with him. He'd get off to jump the man, then get back on the bike with the guy and they'd be away. But the tall man was gripping his briefcase so tight you'd have to break his fingers to get it off him. How much money did he have in it anyway? Only a few thousand yuan, at most. But he was hanging onto it like grim death, even though it wasn't big money.

A couple of cashiers in light blue uniforms were taking a sturdy metal safe stuffed with money to a security van. The slender girls were bent double like the branches of a tree weighed down with fruit. It was a very small safe – 'Packed tight as pancakes' Lexus had said. It was a good image.

Two armed guards marched alongside, their faces half-hidden under steel helmets. The whole long street was full of people staring at the two women with their heavy load. They played up to the crowd, bending over even more. Every eye was on their ritual – a military parade executed with dignity and silent concentration.

They put the safe in the van. They shut the door. It drove off.

Everything went back to normal.

The street lights started to come on, the yellow glare jabbing into my eyes. The streets were full of people and cars, popping up as if they had appeared from another world. They were rolling in money, spending it freely like it was all stolen. But where from? And where was I going? I didn't want to go home, to those four bare walls. I stood looking down the street. A bald man walked by with his arm around a woman who was as slim as those cashiers. He was acting like a real big shot, jabbering away on his mobile phone. A security guard came over from a restaurant, sniffed at me like a dog, then walked away. He had the look of a worried man. A family of three munched their way through a pile of food in the McDonald's opposite, the manageress clearing away the bones they were spitting out on the table. Lights from the passing cars played over her long white fingers.

A car started hooting behind me. It was bearing down on me like a tiger with its jaw gaping wide. I stood my ground.

The horn sounded again. As the car came closer, I could make out the figure of the driver behind the windscreen, talking on his mobile. He hadn't even seen me. He just carried on talking and laughing. What was so important for him, so funny? He must have just robbed someone. Maybe he'd just robbed the cash from that security van. He must have been figuring out how to divide up the loot with his gang. There was no way I was moving. I started gazing leisurely up at the sky. Eventually he shut his phone, stuck his head out of the window and waved me out of the way. I just stood there. He was furious and started roaring at me. I'd always been meek, obedient, the kind of person who'd run away like a frightened cat if someone so much as looked at me. But now I was fearless. The cat had turned into a tiger. I couldn't believe my own bravery. My legs began to tremble. I was causing a traffic jam. The cars were bearing down on me, terrifying me. Horns blared. But I stood right where I was, stubbornly refusing to move. The drivers leaped out of their cars.

'What the hell do you think you're doing, blocking the road?' they yelled. 'Get out of the way! You're holding up traffic. You're contravening traffic regulations, damn it! Just think of the chaos if everybody started standing in the middle of the road.'

'Huh!' I smiled. 'You know nothing about chaos. You've got cars, houses, wives – all stolen. You do exactly what you like yourselves, but you won't have anyone else doing it. We just have to stick to the letter of the law. You say people should abide by the rules, damn right they should. But everyone's cheating and thieving, everyone's at it, everyone's doing exactly what they like. You blame anyone who fiddles the books, but you're happy to line your own pockets. And the big players get let off while the little players get trapped in the net. Only fools get forced into line. I'm no fool, I won't let anyone use me as a stepping-stone for their career. I'm not going to be a scapegoat, no way. No way! I'm going to make you really mad!' But I was the one in a rage, tears blurring my eyes. I slapped the bonnet of the car. 'You think you can hit me because you've got a car? Then go ahead. Run me down!'

7

I started hanging round the Commercial Bank almost every day, checking out the lay of the land, watching the security vans with their metal safes full of bank notes packed tight as pancakes make their morning and evening drop offs. I tried to figure out how Lexus was going to do the job. I was like a meek little lamb, looking up at its mother's teats. He was my lifeline, the source of all my knowledge.

This particular bank was the perfect place for a robbery. There was no space in front or behind and the pavement guard railings went right up to the front door, so the vans had to stop on a side road 50 metres away – I paced it out to be sure. While they were carrying the safes they were the perfect target. Those 50 metres – anything could happen. The guards escorted them every step of the way, but so what? They had guns and uniforms, but could they shoot? They looked pretty hard, of course, their faces as taut as bowstrings. But all you'd have to do was give them a fright. Throw a bomb at them – pow! Shit! I'd make a pretty good robber.

Anyone could rob a bank.

I figured Lexus must have hidden some kind of explosive along the street somewhere, so day after day I searched every nook and cranny. One of my dad's old colleagues found me a job in his company, 800 yuan a month. It was more money than I'd ever earned before, but I turned him down flat. My dad was furious, shouting 'What job are you going to get then? Tell me that?' I just smiled and didn't answer. I didn't need to answer. I went to the Construction Bank every day. That was my job. It was like a pilgrimage. I hung around, trying to work out what Lexus was thinking. I never dreamed of doing the robbery myself, I swear it on Chairman Mao! I was a good man, an honest one. I just wanted to watch, to know if the job would go the way I had imagined, as if there was a prize for getting it right. I didn't even want the prize.

October 1st. National Day.

East Chang'An Avenue was heaving, crawling with police. The air was fragile as a light bulb.

A troop of primary school children came by clutching plastic flowers and flags – a bit of colour for the military parade. They were lined up in front so they could get a good view, their faces shining with happiness. One of them was running backwards and forwards in excitement. He can't have been more than five years old, he'd never seen a parade, never in his entire life. There was so much going on, one fun thing after another. Public holidays always made me happy as a kid. What was the name of that Jason Zhang song: 'I want to tell the future, I feel so brave today ... ' Shane Cao had sung it too.

There was a bicycle halfway down the side street where the security vans used to park. It seemed to come out of nowhere. Very strange. It was old and battered, like a fossil. It stood there on its stand, quiet, profoundly mysterious, as if somehow it would take off into the air as soon as the van arrived.

It arrived!

Fear gripped me.

The streets were jam-packed with people. But the bike didn't move. The sea of heads rippled: two cashiers appeared, as if on the crest of a wave. Two good-looking women in bright outfits standing at the bank's front door. Strange how their uniforms were so bright today. As soon as they came near the bike there would be an explosion, they'd be blown to bits. Even though they were so good-looking. So good-looking it brought me close to tears. They had no idea someone was weeping for them. They strolled blithely past the bicycle. But it didn't move. It hadn't moved an inch. Was the money still in the security van? It must be – the door was still shut. A smile crept over my lips. I hurriedly revised the plot. Lexus had timed the explosion for when the van opened. The doors swung wide. No explosion. How stupid of me! The bomb couldn't go off until the safe was out of the van. Out came the safe. No explosion. Maybe when they got closer. The cashiers picked up the safe and starting heading for the bank, getting closer and closer to the bike. One of their sleeves brushed into it. Still no explosion. The handlebars tilted to one side, as if it was resting. As if it was asleep. What on earth was happening? When was he planning to set it off? Had Lexus forgotten to pack it with explosives? Had something gone wrong with the plan? They'd better sort it out double quick. The fools! The safe was right in front of me. I could read the red lettering. I could reach out and touch it. Go on, go on, somebody grab it! But there was no one there. Where the hell had they got to? It was dead quiet. So quiet it was like I was burning in dry ice.

I could have done the job myself.

Is that what Lexus had meant?

8

After that I was pretty ill.

No sign of Lexus.

One day she came to my house and asked if I'd seen him. I said I hadn't and – to my amazement – she burst into tears. She cried and cried and threw herself on my chest and she slipped both arms under my armpits, and clamped her hands on my shoulder blades. I boldly stroked her arm. She didn't pull away.

Somehow she had fallen in love with me. She said seeing me was like seeing him. But I had no money. I wanted money. I wanted to get married, but how could I make this happen? Day after day I racked my brains. but my mind was a total, terrifying blank.

Go on, rob a bank.

The words slipped out. It was very odd.

There was still no sign of Lexus. Sometimes I even doubted

whether he'd existed. But when she definitely wanted me, she would slip both arms under mine, clamping her hands on my shoulders.

Are you sure about this?
You can shut the book now.
Do you choose to read on?

Our Bones

1

My parents may have been set in their ways, but they always seemed happy. 'Life used to be hell, and now it's good,' they'd say. 'How could we ask for more?' So I never expected them to get into trouble.

It started one evening. My mother was washing the plates. My father was watching the news. Another chorus of economic success. Their lives were better, he supposed, but he'd never bothered to ask himself how.

A voice came through from the kitchen.

'What would you like to eat tomorrow?'

'I don't know,' he said, mystified. 'Anything.'

'Anything?' she laughed. 'What's "anything"?'

She came out of the kitchen and waited for an answer. What an awkward question. He had to answer it all the same.

'Anything means anything,' he said.

'Can't you even name one dish?'

'How do I know?' he snapped. 'What I ate hasn't even gone down the toilet yet. What do you want me to say?'

'What about me!' she flared up. 'I have to decide what we're going to eat 365 days a year. When I go to the supermarket it's like taking an exam.' She had been a teacher, so this was an appropriate image.

She burst into tears. Choosing meals must have been fun once, but now it just felt like a chore. If they tired of eating at home, then they went out: Chinese, then western, then a 'Manchu Imperial Feast', then 'home-style cooking'. When they'd eaten everything there was to eat in the whole wide world, there they were – back to dinner at home again. But what should they eat? Life was certainly better, but choosing what to eat had got more difficult. In the old days, when there wasn't much to eat or drink, everything tasted good.

He went into the kitchen and started on the rest of the washing up. She stopped crying after a while, came in and grabbed a tea towel. He gathered up the clean bowls to put them away but she took them from him with a smile.

It was a brilliant smile which made her look young again. Back then he didn't have time to appreciate her smiles. Like most people, they were short of cash. She tutored and took on extra hours of teaching. He worked long hours at the magazine and parlayed his position as art editor into commissions for painting fans. They lived a spartan life. Only now could they afford to take a bit more care of themselves. How pretty she still was. He told her so.

'Rubbish!' she said. 'I'm an old crone.'

She smiled again. But what could they eat tomorrow?

2

The next morning they decided to go to the supermarket together. They ate a scrappy breakfast, promising themselves to make up for it at lunchtime. They would buy whatever they fancied. The seafood counter teemed with every kind of fish imaginable, more than they could possibly name. But named or unnamed, they'd tried everything on the display at one time or another. The smell made them feel a bit sick. They scurried away.

The meat counter was the noisiest place in the shop, filled with the rhythmic sounds of chopping as the knives rose and fell. One hefty butcher slammed a whole side of pork on to the counter, and started to hack it to bits. He was broad-chested, big-bellied, bare to the waist – one hundred percent slaughterman. Smoke from a cigarette curled up into his half-closed eyes as he disassembled the carcass, wielding the knife with casual grace. One hand attacked while the other dodged in and out, like two dancers. A virtuoso performance of precision and savage strength. He fizzed with energy, like onions in hot oil.

His knife clanged on to the counter and his big, veined hand picked at something in the meat. A bone. The butcher pulled it off the thigh bone and put it to the side. It was a gourd bone.

My father's eyes lit up. My mother tugged at his arm.

She wasn't normally demonstrative in public. It took him back 20 years to when they were first married. There wasn't anything much you could buy as a gift, so he used to go the market and get her a gourd bone – at least that's what the traders called it.

Meat wasn't so easy to buy then, you always needed coupons. You didn't need a coupon to buy bones, but that meant they were always in demand. Thigh bones and pigs' heads went to people with connections, but they got a relative who was a doctor to give them a certificate so they could jump the queue and get a gourd bone at least. They were usually a bit dry and only had the odd shred of meat on them, but my parents made full use of them all the same. They simmered them and scraped off the bits of meat and drank the broth. When the bones had been boiled soft they chewed on them and sucked out the marrow. They were absolutely delicious.

He looked at her and she looked at him and the flavours came flooding back. She could almost see the meat juices dribbling from the corners of his mouth.

'I haven't seen one of those for a long time,' she laughed. 'It's like pigs don't grow with gourd bones any more. I suppose people think they're not worth eating, but people miss out on all sorts of good things.'

The butcher didn't understand what they were after when they asked for a gourd bone. He picked up the thigh bone, thinking they had made some sort of mistake. No one was interested in traditional cuts like pork loin, any more, while the thigh bones kept going up in price.

'No, that one. The one next to it,' she said.

The butcher gave them an odd look and chucked the gourd bone over.

She placed it carefully in the shopping basket.

'How much per pound?' she said.

Even though they could spend what they wanted nowadays, she always asked.

'There's no need to pay,' said the butcher.

'No need to pay?'

'No.'

They couldn't believe it. The butcher waved them away, as if they were beggars.

'What can I charge for this?' he said. 'You want it, you take it.'

'What do you mean?' my father shouted. 'We just want to know how much it is.'

'I said. Nothing.'

'Then we don't want it,' she said.

She grabbed the bone out of her basket and put it back in the middle of the counter, like she wanted to go on bargaining. But the butcher just said 'If you don't want it, don't have it.' He swept the bone on to the floor with his cleaver and carried on chopping meat. They stood there, crestfallen, as the other shoppers elbowed them aside.

3

They fled from the supermarket not knowing what to think, or where to go. They just wandered around the streets. It was nearly noon, and they suddenly became aware that they hadn't fulfilled their promise to their bellies.

They decided to go to a restaurant. The menu had all the usual things on it: seafood, fish, meat, vegetables, noodles, soup. What kind of soup? Clam and frog soup, three-flavour beancurd soup, pickled mustard and shredded pork soup. What about bone soup?

'Yes,' said the waitress. 'Seaweed and spare rib soup.'

'No, thank you.'

'There's yam and thigh bone soup,' she added, 'that has thigh bone in … '

'Do you have gourd bone soup?'

'What?' The waitress looked blank. It was if the word had become obsolete.

'The bit at the top of the thigh bone,' he said, patiently sketching the shape of the bone.

The waitress still didn't understand and went off to call the cook, who came out with a yellow squash in one hand. My father described the bone, pointing at the squash.

'We haven't got that,' the cook said. 'No one wants that nowadays.'

'How come no one wants them?' she asked.

'They're not nutritious,' sniffed the cook. 'Now if you get a thigh bone and boil it all day you get lots of nutrition, even if it's a frozen one.'

'Add a drop of vinegar,' he said. 'That brings the goodness out.'

'I know,' the cook smiled, 'but a gourd bone will never be as nourishing as a thigh bone, even if you add vinegar.'

That really annoyed my father. 'You don't know anything about eating!' he shouted.

'Well, maybe I just know about making it.' The cook was

110

getting cross too. 'You're the one who knows all about eating.'

'I certainly do!' he threw back.

'Then eat, sir!' He turned round and headed back to the kitchen.

They left the restaurant in a rage.

'There's something wrong with the whole world nowadays,' my mother said. 'Did you see the menu? There was nothing worth eating. Just a long list of things with fancy names, all tasting the same.'

'Not half as good as that rice we used to make with soy sauce and a few dried shrimps,' he said. 'Now that was good.'

'Yes. Why don't we have that for lunch?'

They had soy sauce at home, of course, so they bought dried shrimps and fried them up with some rice. But the dried shrimps weren't as good as they used to be – they were too salty – and there was something wrong with the soy sauce as well.

'It's probably made of chemicals,' he said. 'All these damned scientists. That's why everyone's getting cancer.'

He was angry at the whole modern world.

They didn't talk much after that. When they'd finished clearing up she headed off to the bedroom for a nap and he stretched out on the sofa. But he couldn't sleep. He kept thinking of the days when they were young and used to eat those gourd bones.

They'd be huddling around the stove as she washed the bone and put it in the pot, adding water and a few splashes of vinegar. Sour fumes from the simmering broth warmed the room, stinging his eyes – it had to simmer a while. Finally, she took the lid off and the fragrance filled their nostrils. The soup didn't have a lot of fat, all the goodness was in the

111

bone. She took out the bone, scraped off the shreds of meat clinging to it and put them in a bowl, ready for when she was cooking stir-fried vegetables. For the next meal she'd boil the bone up a second time. They'd drink the broth and he'd gnaw on the bone. It was full of flavour. He had good teeth back then, but sometimes he worried about her making a third broth after he'd been chewing on the bone.

'Isn't that unhygienic?' he'd ask.

'Oh for heaven's sake,' she'd say. 'We're family. Do you worry about hygiene when I taste what I'm cooking?'

He'd laugh. No need for a husband and wife to worry about hygiene if they're kissing. That's what love is all about.

The last broth was pale and thin, but a bit of MSG brought it to life. That bone taste … there was nothing like it.

4

They decided to try another supermarket.

Everything was much busier in the evening, with noise and bustle spilling out on to the pavement. The one they chose had a makeshift stage at the entrance for a singer and a raffle. A salesman stopped them as they went in.

'Take a look at this colour TV, sir.'

My father brushed him off and walked on.

'If you don't look, you'll never know if you like it. Take a look, sir, it's HD.'

He tried to ignore him, but the salesman leaped in front

of him, blocking his way.

'What's all this about?' she said. 'We don't want one.'

'You don't want a good TV? Then what do you want?'

'We've already got a colour TV,' she said.

'Of course you do,' said the salesman. 'I know just what kind of TV a pair of old folks like you have at home. Why don't you trade it in for a new one?'

My father stopped and looked round at the salesman, who cheerfully started in on his sales patter. But my mother butted in: 'We don't want to get a new TV, we don't need one.'

'Nowadays people get a new one as soon as they see one they like. Look at the colours, sir, look at the flat screen … '

The salesman grabbed at my father's arm, but he shoved him away, hard. He never knew he was so strong. He was a painter, not a boxer, but maybe all those years of practising calligraphy had been good for something after all.

'OK, so you don't want it.' The man steadied himself. 'There's no need to hit me.'

'You just got in our way,' she said.

'This is where we lay out the goods. Right here, in front of the supermarket. We're not in their way. So you're better than this supermarket are you? They've got absolutely everything in there … '

'So have we,' she said. 'Your rotten old TVs aren't worth looking at.'

'These are top of the range: super-size screen, back projection,' pointing them out to the crowd that had gathered round, 'film projector, home cinema. An entire cinema in your home.' The salesman raised his voice. 'Isn't that enough? Are none of these worth looking at?'

'No!'

'You don't know what you're missing out on. You have no idea.'

'Of course I do. We just don't want one.' my father replied.

'You mean you can't afford one,' the salesman sneered. 'Nobody doesn't want things, they just don't have the money.'

My mother held my father back as he went scarlet with rage. Some of the bystanders started asking the salesman what business it was of his if the old couple couldn't afford a new TV and telling my parents that they shouldn't take any notice. Now my father wanted to buy the most expensive TV in the display, just to show the salesman that he was not a man to be messed with. But that would be admitting that the TV was worth having. And what if it was a rip-off? Then he'd really look like a fool.

Caught up by the crowd of shoppers, they stumbled into the supermarket, watched by countless eyes. What were they after? A gourd bone. There was nothing to be ashamed of.

They marched up to the butchers' counter, but there was only a woman cleaning up and a few pre-wrapped chunks of meat.

'Where can we get gourd bones?' they asked.

The cleaner didn't understand.

She re-phrased the question: 'Where can we get bones?'

'None left.'

'There must be,' he said.

The cleaner pointed to the rubbish bins behind the counter. There on top of the discarded fat and gristle were a couple of gourd bones. My mother leaned over, pulled them out, put them in a bag and placed them in her shopping basket. People were giving them strange glances, as if they were a couple of beggars.

Paying suddenly became terribly important. Once you picked up your meat from the counter, you were supposed to get it weighed and stick on a bar code. Standing in the queue they felt like real shoppers, but the girl refused to serve them.

'That stuff's not for sale,' she said.

'What do you mean, not for sale?' They acted confused.

'They're not for sale,' the girl repeated.

'But we want to buy them,' my father said loudly.

'Well, you can't.'

'Just tell us the price, please.' My mother was almost begging.

'We don't set the prices here,' said the girl. 'I don't have a price for these, so I can't tell you how much it is.'

They slunk away, muttering to each other.

'Why do they need a bar code anyway?' she said. 'It's almost as if it's more important than the goods they're trying to sell. They've got it all backwards.'

Then she had an idea. The cleaner had finished at the butchers' counter, but there were still two pre-wrapped pieces of meat sitting there. The labels didn't say what kind of meat it was. One was heavier than the other. More expensive. She peeled the bar code off the more expensive cut and stuck it on the bag of bones. Then she scuttled quickly away, stifling her laughter behind her hands like a little kid. She wished she was still a kid. My father wagged his finger at her and pretended to chase her, but she hadn't done anything bad. In fact, quite the opposite. She certainly hadn't ripped anyone off. She was making money for the supermarket.

They skipped the weighing desk and went straight to the

check out. The cashier stifled a yawn, took the bag of bones and scanned it in. They almost jumped for joy as they heard the register beep. But just as the exhausted cashier was putting it into the carrier bag, the sharp end of the bone poked through and snagged on the handles. The cashier pushed it in a little then stopped, took the packet out and had a good look. How could someone so tired ever notice something like that?

'This isn't right,' said the cashier.

'Why not?' he countered.

'It doesn't match the bar code.'

'How do you know?' my mother scoffed. 'You can't see what's in the pack and there's nothing written on the label.'

'Of course I can see. It's not for sale.'

'Not for sale? But we want to buy it.'

'Well you can't. I can't process the sale.'

'Really?' She said, giving the bar code a poke.

'That's not the right price,' said the cashier.

'So tell us how much it is,' she said, getting out a wad of notes and putting them on the counter.

The cashier picked up the money, but she didn't unfold the notes, she handed them straight back. My parents refused to take them, hoping the cashier would accept the money and put it in her till. But she just dropped the notes on the counter. My mother recoiled from them as if they'd given her an electric shock. My father pushed them away. They lay on the counter, useless and abandoned.

'What do you think you're doing?' the cashier shouted, tired and irritable.

'We want to buy it,' he shot back. 'And we've got the money.'

'What makes you think it's OK just because you've got

116

money?' The cashier flared up. 'You think money will buy you anything?'

'That's just the way it is nowadays.' He was angry too. 'If you've got the money, anything's possible.'

The manager came hurrying over and looked at the packet.

'It's our mistake,' he said, 'this bone's been put in the wrong package. I'm sorry for the inconvenience. We just can't get the staff nowadays.' He raised his voice. 'They have no respect for the customers.'

My mother trembled. 'Are you having a go at me?' she shouted.

'No.' The manager was amazed. 'What's the problem?'

'You shouldn't be having a go at anyone.' she said.

'Ah, you thought I was accusing you.' The penny dropped. 'You got hold of these bones yourselves. A pair of old folks like you. You know what that is, don't you? It's stealing, it's a crime.'

'Me? Steal? But I was paying over the odds.'

'That's still stealing,' said the manager. 'And who the hell knows what kind of sinister plan you're cooking up. We should take you down to the police station. That'll sort you out.'

The only time my parents had been to the police was when a classmate of my mother's had been caught shoplifting. They turned to flee.

'Hey! Take your money!' the manager shouted.

They didn't care about leaving the money even though they hadn't taken the gourd bones. They didn't care about the bones. But the security guards caught up with them and stuffed the wad of notes into their hands, saying 'What on earth do you think you're doing?'

5

'That was all your fault! All your stupid idea!' he turned on his wife.

'Did you have a better one?' she snapped.

'Maybe I'm stupid too,' he said, 'with all this useless money.' He threw the wad of notes to the ground. 'Look at all the money I've earned. But what good is it now?'

He punched himself on the head. She grabbed his arm to try and stop him, but he carried on punching harder and harder, as if he was trying to brain himself.

So she let go. 'Fine. Go ahead. Do yourself in. And I will too. We'll die together.'

That evening he couldn't get to sleep. He sat there on the sofa, memories of the old days going round and round in his head. There was no problem buying gourd bones back then.

My mother hadn't been well. She was pregnant and had to eat nutritious food, like bone broth, but she wouldn't drink it all herself. She always tried to insist he should have some too, until they ended up pushing the pot back and forth between them.

'I can always chew the bone,' he said.

'So can I,' she said.

'But what about your teeth? Your bones are all weak because you're pregnant.'

'My teeth are fine.'

'What about our child? You're not just eating for yourself.'

'The child doesn't matter,' she said. 'My stomach hurts, I can't eat any more. I feel sick.'

'OK, throw it away then. Go on, throw it away! If you don't eat that bone, I'll stick it in the bin!'

He grabbed it and shouted and waved it around in the air and tapped her on the head with it until she burst into tears, and so did he.

How he longed to eat a gourd bone one more time, even if it did lead to a row.

In the middle of the night he got up to go to the toilet. When he turned on the light in the hall he found a burglar trying to get into the study. Fear shot through him, but then he remembered there was nothing worth stealing. It was almost as if getting burgled showed they were worth something after all.

The burglar turned to run away, but my father told him to stop. He put his finger to his lips, so he wouldn't wake my mother, then said: 'If you reckon there's anything of value, just take it.'

The burglar was rooted to the spot.

'You could squash an old man like me between your fingers like an ant. What are you afraid of?'

My father went into the bedroom, got the key and unlocked the study, standing back to let the burglar in. He turned the light on. Still the burglar didn't move. Maybe the house was full of too much stuff. They'd been gathering things for years. Or maybe the burglar thought it was a trap. And what was there to take anyway? It was all rubbish.

He went in himself, opened a drawer and took out some money. It was only a few hundred yuan, which they kept at home in case they needed a bit of cash. He held it out. But the burglar eyed him suspiciously and didn't take it.

'It's not enough?' he said.

He got out a couple of savings books and his ID card, and told the burglar the PIN number for his bank account. The burglar couldn't believe it. He shot a fierce, mistrustful glance around the room.

'I know, I know,' he said. 'it's not that much. But it's still money, you can buy yourself something to eat ... '

The burglar didn't say a word.

'Do you want it or not?' my father shouted. The burglar turned and ran.

My father followed him to the door but he had gone. He sat down on the doorstep until it got light and my mother came to find him.

'It's better to be a burglar,' he said.

'What?'

'You can do what you want if you're a burglar,' he said. 'You come and go whenever you like and if you don't want anything, you just leave. It's better to be a burglar.'

'Whatever gave you that idea?'

She hadn't got much sleep either. She dreamed she had to march through the street with a tall hat on her head, just like in the Cultural Revolution. Not that it ever happened to her. They were both Red Guards back then, like everybody else.

'It's like we're no good,' he said. 'Everyone pushes us around.'

6

They couldn't believe there was nowhere in the city, nowhere in a country as vast as China where they could get hold of some gourd bones, so they decided to try a farmer's market. There was no way a small trader would refuse money – they'd do anything to make a quick buck.

As soon as they got to the market they spotted two gourd bones on a butcher's stall.

'We'd like those bones,' my mother said – she didn't want to say 'buy'.

The stallholder laughed, his round face creasing into a broad smile.

'You remember those?' he asked. Finally they'd found someone who understood. Maybe he'd eaten them as a child.

'Back then you could only get hold of them if you were sick,' she said.

'Exactly,' said the butcher. 'But those days are long gone. Things are so much better now.'

'Yes … I suppose,' she said. 'But these bones, for instance, how come no one wants them now?'

'Well, if you want them, just take them.'

'How much do you want to sell them for?' she stammered.

'I'm not selling them. If you want them, take them,' the stallholder insisted, with a dismissive wave of his hand.

He was just trying to get rid of them.

Chen Xiwo

'No,' my father said, 'we want to buy them!'

'You can't.'

'We've got money.'

The butcher laughed again. 'You don't need much money to buy these.'

'What do you mean?'

'These bones are worth nothing. If you've got money, there are plenty of ways to spend it.'

'But we want to spend it here.'

'If you really want to buy them, just give me anything you want.'

Finally he was going to take their money. My father said quickly: 'How much?'

The stallholder scratched his head. 'OK, how about one yuan.'

'One yuan? One yuan each?'

'Of course not. Are you crazy? One yuan for both of them.'

'That's too cheap. It's like giving them away.'

'But there isn't a price for them. Look – there's nothing to eat on them.'

'Yes there is,' they said together.

'Well, maybe that's what you think. But I can't just sell them like that ... that would be illegal, wouldn't it?'

'So what if it's illegal.' She couldn't believe the words had slipped out.

'What are you saying, missus, what do you mean?' The butcher's face darkened. These customers were just making trouble – best have nothing to do with them. He picked up his cleaver and started chopping up a joint.

'I'm so sorry,' she stammered, 'that's not what I meant ... we just want to buy the bones.'

'Just take them.'

'But they're too cheap,' she protested, 'only 50 cents each!'

'What do you think they are?' the butcher shouted. 'Human skulls?'

They shivered, suddenly uneasy.

'We want the skulls,' my father said.

'Hey, don't say things like that … get out of here. Get out of here both of you, leave me alone.'

They didn't move.

'We want the skulls!' he shouted.

The butcher rushed out from behind his counter and tried to shove them away, but they stood firm, because otherwise it would all be over, otherwise they'd be condemned to a life of mediocrity. They stood there, on the margins between life and death, battling for their principles.

How could a couple of old people be so strong?

'OK, OK.' The stallholder gave in. 'Just pay me whatever you like.'

But what were gourd bones really worth nowadays? They were willing to pay anything to fulfil their dream, but they had no idea how much 'anything' actually was. In the old days a gourd bone cost five cents, but incomes had gone up 30 times since then. So five cents times 30: one and a half yuan.

'Three yuan the pair,' she said.

'OK, OK,' said the butcher, waving his hand in defeat. 'Just take them away. And don't you go telling the Department of Industry and Commerce I ripped you off.'

'Of course we wouldn't,' she said.

'Go on then. Get lost.'

They put the money on the counter. The stallholder didn't even look at it.

7

They set off home, happily clutching their precious gourd bones. As she fumbled for her change on the steps of the bus, she put the bag down by the ticket machine.

'Take those off!' yelled the driver. 'Filthy, nasty things.'

'What do you mean?' said my father. 'Don't you know what they are?'

'They're bones, aren't they?' said the driver.

'Yes,' he said, 'but what kind of bones?'

'They're just bones,' said the driver. 'They're not worth anything.'

'And how much do you think they cost?' my mother asked.

'You tell me,' the driver shot back.

Three yuan altogether. Not even as much as a couple of bus fares. They took their seats in silence.

After a while he blurted out: 'We didn't pay enough.'

'We should have paid a bit more. How can you use income to work it out? Prices have gone up much faster than income over the last 20 years, but how can you calculate it with price increases? It's impossible.'

'We didn't think,' he said. 'He gave them to us almost for free.'

'It was as if he was giving us charity,' she declared.

'But we don't need charity. Huh, how ridiculous!'

They decided to leave the bag of bones on the bus, but

when they got home they were bereft. They had wanted to buy some gourd bones so much, but as soon as they got hold of them, they abandoned them. They felt empty and foolish. How had they got into such a mess? No one else was so serious about anything nowadays. The pragmatic solution was to go back to the supermarket and buy some bones – any old bones. Spare ribs would do, or even a piece of pork loin if they couldn't get ribs. When they got there the butcher wouldn't just sell them the bones, they had to buy the meat too. But all they did was cut off the meat and throw it away. It was the most wasteful thing they'd ever done.

She simmered the bones and made a broth. A pungent smell of vinegar wafted up.

'We have gourd bone soup!' she cried as she carried it to the table.

It was just like the old days. What a magician she was, taking spare rib and transforming it into fragrant gourd bone soup.

She performed the little ritual from the old days, carrying the enamel basin around the table as if she was dancing a ballet or making a spell which transformed the lowly bones into a pure meat soup. But now she had transformed a meat soup into a bone broth. And it was much more delicious. The broth had the power to seep into every taste bud and release the gastric juices.

'Pork loin soup, spare rib soup, thigh bone soup, none of them are a patch on gourd bone soup,' he cried.

Everyone wanted pork loin back then. At works dinners, their colleagues' eyes glinted like leopards' when a dish with meat was carried out. Everyone thrust their spoons into the bowl and stirred it around, desperate to scoop up a few morsels of meat with the broth. Nobody wanted to be too obvious about it. They used to swirl their spoons around in the bowl, pretending to talk. But their spoons went rat-a-tat-tat against the sides of the bowl in search of meat, like an exchange of gunfire.

'When I look back, the more hardship we suffered, the more fun it was,' he said. 'Oh I know we were very poor, but we were so young. Remember the heavy guns we carried in military training? We worked all day, studied politics in the evenings and we laboured in the fields too, "emulating Lei Feng", "preparing against war and natural disasters", digging air raid shelters, dredging rivers, all sorts of patriotic volunteering work. Once you even fainted on the river bed.'

They burst out laughing. Life had been hard back then but, looking back, she had happy memories. There was something romantic about those days ...

'That must have been how we got the certificate to buy the bones,' she said. 'One of the district leaders said "We've got to look after this good, hard-working comrade," and she made our work unit do me a letter saying I needed meat.'

'And what use was that letter to you?' He pulled a wry face. 'You only wangled a sick note because I managed to get hold of that great-uncle of mine who was a doctor.'

'So you're quite capable of lying,' she teased.

But he had no problem admitting he had lied, or even that he'd broken the law.

'If I hadn't lied, would you be here today?' he said.

'No, I wouldn't,' she nodded.

'I remember the first time we went to buy bones with the sick note,' he said. 'You wouldn't let me go on my own, so we got up together at the crack of dawn on a freezing cold winter's morning – we were worried there might be none left. We drank some hot water to warm us inside and off we went, terrified we'd make a mess of it and get found out and they'd arrest us.' The colour drained from their faces at the memory. He patted her shoulder and went on. 'We went to the meat counter to pay … No, that's not right. I went alone, so you could stay in the background in case I needed back-up. If they thought I had a fake sick note, I'd need your help to escape.'

The mystery and excitement of their former crime filled them with courage, firing them up even though they were now frail and old. He carried on with the story.

'We saw some bones on the counter. Some had more meat on them than others, like the thigh bone, which at least had marrow inside. There were pigs' heads, with all sorts of bits you could eat between the skull bones – the brains, the palate, the eyeballs. But what would they sell us? I spotted a bone at the very end of the counter, a gourd bone. "I want … that one … " I said. The butcher looked up. I jumped. Good heavens, what a glare! But I couldn't back out now, because retreat would make him even more suspicious. So I screwed up my courage and said again: "I want… that one … ".'

'"Five cents," he said. Just like that … I could hardly believe it. I started nodding, like a hen pecking at rice. And he threw the bone into my wicker basket. That's right, we still used wicker baskets. Where did ours get to? Everyone talks about the government's shopping basket programme but it's all plastic bags these days … '

'What are you going on about?' she asked, impatient. 'Get to the point.'

'OK,' he said. 'Well, I grabbed my basket and was about

to set off when the butcher shouted: "The money!"'

'"Oh, I forgot. I completely forgot," I said, panic-stricken. We were nearly done for. If he thought I was trying to leave without paying, that would have been it, wouldn't it? We'd have been done for. As quick as I could I pulled out my money and handed it over – I think I gave him a bit too much. But he handed me back the correct change. He didn't spot the fake sick note and he didn't overcharge me. We'd done it. A successful heist. I went off with my basket, my gourd bone and a wad of notes. As if I'd robbed a bank. I turned round and smiled at you.'

'I was watching, I was so worried,' she said.

'I know, I know,' he said.

'It was amazing,' she said. 'There was someone standing beside me, looking at me very strangely. I thought he must be a policeman, a plain clothes one. I hid behind a pillar and peered out. Then I strolled over to the vegetable stall opposite, acting like nothing was up, going from this pillar to that one, until I finally lost him. I was all ready to start running. If anything had happened to you, I'd have been right over, protecting you, helping you get away.

'Yes, I know,' he said. 'But if you'd been arrested, what then?'

'What would they arrest me for? I hadn't broken any law, I'd done nothing.'

'You were my accomplice,' he said. 'I was the main offender, but you were my accomplice.'

'Well, maybe I was,' she said, looking uncommonly roguish for a former teacher.

He laughed out loud. 'You're a bad woman.'

'And what about you?' she said. 'If you hadn't been bad,

we wouldn't be here today, we'd have starved to death.'

She tapped the side of the bowl before them, full to the brim with soup she had just made. The bowl rang out, the broth rippling to reveal rib bones. Rib bones, not gourd bones. Their faces fell. They'd wangled a fake sick note and scared themselves silly to get hold of them in the old days, but now gourd bones were worth nothing at all. Now they were discarded as if they were only rubbish.

'Let's go and steal some,' she said.

'What?' She wasn't joking.

It was as if he hardly knew her, as if she was a stranger – just like the first time he set eyes on her. He'd really fallen for her, would have gone to hell and back at her command. So they'd go and steal some gourd bones. At least that way the bones would be worth something.

8

The market where they'd bought the gourd bones 20 years before had been pulled down, burying their memories under a tide of urban development, so they found another covered market built in the old style. Walking among the forest of pillars, it was as if they were putting together a dramatic reconstruction of their old crime.

They'd brought along a wicker basket, though they had trouble getting hold of that as well. Eventually they found one in a theatrical shop. The owner asked what play they were putting on. They smiled but didn't answer.

The market was crowded, the food piled high for New Year. With just one more day to go before the festivities, people were spending as if it was the end of the world. But New Year meant nothing to my parents as they shuffled lonely through the frenzy of the market. Or perhaps it meant everything – they had to steal a gourd bone to make it through another year.

A strong westerly blew through the pillars. She stroked her husband's sleeve.

'I told you to put a jumper on, but you wouldn't listen,' she said.

'I'm not cold,' he answered. He never used to wear many clothes back then, partly because he was a tough lad, but partly because he couldn't afford them.

'You never give up,' she said. 'Even though you've been treated badly your whole life.' She was getting into her stride. 'We both have ... and what for? What was the point of earning all this money?'

She took his hand. He didn't care if people laughed at them, holding hands like pair of teenagers. People had always laughed at them. Let them laugh.

'I don't like wearing too many clothes,' he said.

'What do you like, then?'

He couldn't think what to say.

'I'd like to be a beggar,' he declared.

'Haven't we been beggars all our lives? And never given a fair chance. And now we have to start stealing things.'

Besides, a voice cried in their ears, this isn't stealing, this is resisting. The words seemed to blast at them from loudspeakers, just like they did 30 years ago on their first action as Red Guards. They had burst into a teacher's house with all the others and ransacked it from top to bottom, with the loudspeakers blaring: 'This is revolution! The revolution is justified! It's right to rebel!'

They spotted three gourd bones on a butcher's stall, lying right at the end of the counter. There was a crush of people around the stall, the stall-holder chopping up the meat and totting up the money at lightning speed. Every now and then, he raised his head to look for his wife, grumbling that she had been off delivering meat to a hotel for ages. This was their moment. ~~~~~~~~~~ dodged behind a pillar. My father elbowed his way to the counter and held the wicker basket underneath, out of the stallholder's sight. All he needed to do was reach out his hand and sweep the gourd bones towards him. He turned to smile in her direction and reached towards them. But just then the butcher's wife came back.

He quickly drew back his hand.

Now there were two pairs of eyes. He looked around again for my mother. She was stamping her feet with worry. But tomorrow was New Year's Day. It was now or never.

Suddenly the stallholder shouted: 'We're out of change!' His wife grabbed a hundred-yuan note and rushed away. My father looked around again at my mother.

He nodded.

He reached out and swept the bones off the counter. They landed in the wicker basket with a clatter that seemed to echo around the market. The butcher whirled round. My father went white as a sheet, his eyes full of panic, then turned and fled. The stallholder yelled and leaped from behind the counter, knocking over his stand and the till with it. Remembering the part she had played all those years ago, my mother blocked the butcher's path and watched as my father leaped forwards through the crowds like a man much younger than his years. Like the young man he was when he was courting her. But the stallholder cut in where there were fewer people on the right-hand side, and was right on his heels.

'This way!' she shouted, launching herself towards him and grabbing the basket.

Off she ran, the basket clasped in her arms. What teamwork. The bystanders stood gaping, astonish∙∙∙ ∙∙∙ ∙r by their shop-lifting skills or th∙∙ ∙∙∙ ∙∙∙ ∙∙ to let them through, then closing i∙ ∙∙ ∙∙∙ ∙∙∙ ∙ get a proper look after they had passed. Caught in the crowds the butcher howled in frustration until someone shouted: 'Call the police! Call the police!'

9

The police wound up calling me. Not because they'd arrested my parents, but because my parents refused to walk free. As soon as he found out that the only things they'd taken were some worthless gourd bones, the sergeant wanted to let them go.

'Then why did you arrest us in the first place?' said my mother.

'Because you took something that didn't belong to you,' the policeman said.

'So that's stealing then. Theft.'

'No!' the sergeant shouted. 'It's just a few bones no one wanted. They're worth nothing.'

'What we did was worth nothing?' she yelled back. 'Everything we've done has been worth nothing? We've been through so much, suffered so much, been treated unfairly all our lives. And it's not worth a cent? We suffered it all for nothing? Just you listen … ' And she started on her usual litany of complaints, counting them off on her fingers:

When they were born, the country was in chaos.

They grew up during the Three Years of 'Natural Disasters'.

The Cultural Revolution wrecked their school years, branding them rebels and banishing them to remote villages.

When they married, they were too poor to afford even a quilt.

The children were born and grew up.

They were lucky enough to get to university, where they had to study like crazy because of the Four Modernisations.

But when they tried to get a job, people with degrees were earning less than manual workers.

So they had to work abroad until they made some money.

Life was hard in the old days. This was how people had suffered. People who only ever wanted a better life.

'That's enough, Mum,' I said.

'Don't interrupt,' she said. 'If we hadn't suffered so much, would you be here today? If we hadn't got those gourd bones, would you be alive now?'

I'd never seen a gourd bone, never even heard of one. But this humble bone had fortified the miraculous broth which had made me big and strong.

Back at the market where my parents had committed their

crime, I found one on a butcher's stall, sticking up just like a gourd. A pig scapula. There are all sorts of peculiar bones in every animal, high or low. They never notice them when they are young and healthy, but as they grow old they begin to ache and creak. I had to buy one.

Are you sure about this?
You can shut the book now.
Do you choose to read on?

I Love M

1. The Crime

I didn't realise how many people I'd piss off when I started as head of the vice squad. It was my job to keep the streets clean, of course, but when we rounded up a bunch of hostesses from a nightclub, all hell was let loose. Without the sex industry, entertainment businesses took a hit and that was bad for hotels. With the hotels half empty, nobody went out at nights, so taxi drivers started cruising the city like vengeful ghosts, hitting their steering wheels and cursing the authorities. The traffic police were down on fines, the commerce department was down on admin charges, finance was down on taxes. Everyone was out of pocket, and my boss was pissed off too.

'The sex industry is a pillar of our city's economy,' he fumed. 'Don't you want the city to get rich? If we want the economy to develop, we have to make the best use of whatever we have to hand. And what we have to hand is prostitutes. You've got to let them go.'

Those girls knew the score. They took their sweet time getting their things together, fixing their makeup, doing their hair. I told them they had to find a different way of making y gave me spoke volumes.

ve you're only interested in selling your

pursued.

ur bodies are a gift from our parents,' one put in. 'Just like yours made you one metre eighty tall, so you can arrest bad girls like us.'

'I don't arrest bad girls because I'm tall.' I looked stern. 'I arrest people for a reason.'

Of course, in this job my size and strength are – quite literally – big assets. When I arrest someone they look guilty even if they're innocent. On my beat, if grown-ups want to scare their kids they say 'I'll get One Eighty to lock you up.'

My nickname was a wedding present. My wife's family was well off and there were plenty of other men who fancied her, but she only wanted me. At the wedding, people asked her why she had chosen me. She smiled but said nothing. A colleague cleared his throat and ventured, 'Is it because he's one metre eighty tall?' From that time on, I was known as One Eighty.

My parents gave me a fine physique and a bright future. When I sat the exams for the police academy, they went easy on me at the interview. At athletics meetings, I always carried the flag. In college shows, I always played the hero. Women look at me with frank admiration. The imposing stature my parents gave me is a gift I can never repay.

But I couldn't get my head around this new murder case. The victim was a woman in her fifties. The main suspect was none other than her son.

He was a cripple.

He sat there on the bed, his body twisted from the polio he had as a kid. I told one of my officers to help him up, but as soon as the suspect was upright, he keeled over. His legs were useless.

'You'll have to carry him out,' said a neighbour.

So I picked him up and put him in the car. How could he be the killer?

'His mother carried him everywhere on her back,' said another. 'He couldn't even stand with a stick.'

Why had his mother let him beat her to death? If she had just moved a bit, he wouldn't even have got near her. Her body was covered with lash marks from a leather whip we found with a soft sheath around the handle, made from rags. The stitching was so fine I couldn't even feel the seams. But he went everywhere on his mother's back. How could he have got hold of it?

The neighbours said they'd only heard one cry, like someone letting air out of a balloon. The door stayed closed. The grocer next door had pressed his ear to the wall and thought he heard a whip. But no groans. Surely you would make a noise if someone was beating you to death?

'Round here it's all shacks,' the grocer added, 'the walls are so thin you can sometimes see shadows through them. But not this one. They had wallpaper.'

They had kept themselves to themselves. The head of the residents' committee was the last person to go and see them. The mother stood in the doorway, a rancid smell flooding from the room behind her.

'If anything's up, just call us,' the woman said.

'Call you for what?' asked the mother.

So no one called again. The committee was too busy with family planning, rubbish collection, the neighbourhood song and dance troupe. They always put on a good show when there was a festival or some campaign. But the cripple and his mother never got involved.

Her husband had died long ago, when she was only thirty, but she never married again, because of her son. He got polio when he was two. The experts said there was no cure, but his mother tied his legs to wooden boards to try and help him walk, or strapped him to the bedpost to exercise his back. She used to make him do it for hours every day, until he was in pain, exhausted, beads of sweat trickling down his face.

'If he doesn't do this now, what kind of life will he have?' she used to say.

Her neighbours tried to persuade her to ease off.

'It's not doing any good,' they said.

'We can't give up,' she insisted. 'We've got to keep trying.'

But it was no use. She had to carry him everywhere – on her back, in her arms, any way she could – even when he was grown up. Sometimes he hung round her neck, or clung to her back, or even hung on to her breasts.

She used to work in a factory, but it closed down. She put her severance pay in a savings account so it didn't get frittered away and carried on working. She'd do some cleaning in the mornings and then rush home to make lunch for her son. She was only fifty, but it was hard work and she began to worry what would happen to her son when she was too old to carry on. She decided that she had to find him a wife.

She asked the man she cleaned for to help her out. At first he couldn't think what kind of girl to introduce to a cripple. She'd have to be able to look after him, of course, so she'd have to be strong and she couldn't be an idiot. But it didn't really matter what she looked like. In the end he found an ugly girl, a real minger. He told her that her future husband's legs were a bit stiff, but he could walk a bit. When she found he couldn't even stand up, she turned them down flat.

Next he tried someone from the country – if a girl was poor enough she'd do anything to escape. He came back from a remote village in Sichuan with a beautiful girl. Everyone thought she was wonderful, but one day the mother stumbled out of the house, yelling that their deposit book and their ID cards were gone. The girl had taken them and cleared out their savings. Turned out she'd given them a false address as well.

Now they didn't even have a dowry.

The mother started getting bruises. She'd greet her neighbours with a good morning and a cheery smile, but her face was covered in marks. The neighbours were not surprised. A mother gives her child everything, and her only fear is having nothing to give. A mother would cut flesh from her body for her son to eat. They tried to intervene, but the mother said 'It doesn't matter. Let him hit me, if it makes him feel better.'

There was an old guy who lived a few streets away with his retarded daughter. She was violent too. When she got angry she'd hit her father so hard he'd run across the street and swear at her. Someone made a crack about their two households being well matched, but the mother took it seriously. She went and cooked for the old man. She did his washing and looked after his simple daughter. She brought her son round on her back and made him play with the daughter, even though she barely had the brains of a three year old.

How could a retard look after a cripple? But the mother wasn't that stupid. She was counting on the two of them having a child. When the child grew up, it could look after the disabled parents.

The plan went wrong the night she moved her quilt to the old man's bedroom. Her son was in with the daughter on a mattress laid out on the floor, but the retard got bored of playing with him and dragged him out of her room like a dead dog. She left him in the middle of the street, blocking the road, and when a truck couldn't get past the driver woke all the neighbours with his horn. They peered out of their windows and saw the cripple dragging himself along in the dirt, his neck rigid with effort as the girl shouted 'Go away! I don't want to play with you any more.'

His mother begged on her hands and knees, but she refused to have him back. That girl must have had some smarts because she ran to a telephone box and called the cops. They carted him off in a car. The neighbours said that his legs thrashed about under the cop's arm but his eyes were full of despair. They didn't see much of them after that.

2. The Interrogation

Some suspects deny all charges. Some play dumb, others play the innocent. But I'd never met a suspect who simply ignored me. He couldn't look at you straight, he had to screw up his face and squint sideways, but as he sat there in the interview room his gaze was fixed off to one side, as if he was already somewhere else.

With his mother dead, there was no one left to look after

him. He couldn't eat, he couldn't go to bed, he couldn't piss or shit without help, so the cleaners had to do everything for him while he was locked up. They made a fuss about it all right, but when they helped him go to the toilet they'd say, 'Aiya, that guy's cock is huge.'

But I didn't care about his cock. I just wanted him to confess.

I watched him in his cell one night, thinking he might drop his guard. He was writhing about on the floor, banging his head against the wall, sobbing maybe – I guess if you'd killed your mother you'd be sorry, no matter what. He struggled frantically, like a dying animal, and called out 'Mum!' His whole body suddenly shook and he was still. He looked like he was dead.

After a long time, he propped himself up on one arm, flopped over and groped blindly for the wall. He stretched out a hand and rubbed the wall. Then he lay down again and let out a long sigh.

When we went to fetch him the next day for a court appearance, the wall was covered in spunk. The whole cell reeked of it, that male smell of sex. It was revolting. An officer dragged him straight to the interview room.

'What were you doing last night?' I shouted

No answer.

'You did nothing?'

'What am I supposed to have done?'

'I'm asking you.'

'I didn't do anything!'

'Then what's that on the wall?'

'Nothing.'

'I just went in your cell.'

141

Grin.

'What is that stuff?'

'Snot.'

'Liar. Let me remind you. We'll go easier on you if you're straight with us. Screw us around and you're in big trouble. Tell us the truth.'

'About what?'

'You wanked off!'

He looked down.

'I didn't.'

'Didn't what?'

'I just didn't.'

I needed him to say it. He had to say it. He was ready to talk. I had picked at his scab and now it was bleeding. He glared at me and jerked his head like a chicken being strangled.

'What makes you think you're so great,' he shouted, 'with your arms and your legs?'

'I am an officer of the law,' I answered.

'And what if you were a cripple?'

'I wouldn't murder people. I wouldn't murder my mother.'

'Shut up.'

'Did she kill herself then?' I sneered. 'What did you kill her for?'

'We couldn't live together.'

'You got angry?'

'I hated her.'

'Why? Was it her fault you were a cripple?'

'Yes!' he shouted.

He didn't say anything more. He just sat there rocking back and forth with his arms as if he wanted to get up and go. He swayed from one side to the other, then slid to the floor with a groan. I called in the cop who had brought him. The cripple scrambled on to his back like a child, desperate to get away.

'You hated her, didn't you?' I shouted. 'Is it because she stopped you wanking?'

The cop put him back on the chair.

'Did your mother find out about your disgusting habit?'

He didn't answer.

'So you're not going to talk,' I said. 'Fine. But you killed her because you hated her.'

'I didn't hate her!' he shouted. 'I didn't hate my mum!'

His whole body shook as he glared at me, choking with fury. He gave a hoarse cry, his eyes bulging, and then slumped back, gasping for breath with his face dangling backwards over the chair as if his throat was cut.

'You hated her,' I said. 'You hated your mother, and so you killed her.'

He didn't deny it.

'Because she gave birth to you?'

He nodded.

'If she couldn't make me happy, why have me?' he said.

'But you didn't get sick until you were two years old.'

'She should have killed me then.' He gave an odd laugh. 'One shake and that would have been it. A grown-up is stronger, it's harder to die.'

'Stop thinking about death.'

'Easy for you to say. You can have whatever you want. A job, a wife … '

'You could too,' I said. But I knew that wasn't true.

'Yes, I could,' he said and laughed again. 'But what kind of girl would she be? I've met the ugliest, stupidest girls in the world. Why would I want to get hitched to one of them? My mum said I should get married, because that's what normal people do. But I'm not normal, am I.'

'You didn't want to get married?'

'No way.'

'You don't need to?'

'Nope.'

'Really?'

He looked at me, his face twisted in vicious grimace.

'I can have a wank,' he said. 'Just like you.'

I couldn't admit to that. I'm a cop.

'Don't talk rubbish,' I bellowed.

'You're a man too.' He laughed. 'You're just like me.'

'Rubbish!' I'd said it again.'You been at it long, have you?'

'Not to begin with.'

'So when did you start?'

'The night the cops picked me up off the street,' he said. 'That was the first time. Can you imagine how it felt? After they dropped me home, I couldn't stop thinking about it.'

I nodded.

'In the middle of the night I woke with a hard-on. I couldn't come. I couldn't dream either. There was just reality. And the reality was, my life was empty. Nothing except for a room, a bed. But the bed wasn't empty, because my mother was in it … ' he twitched nervously and fell silent.

'I know,' I said.

'You know what?'

'I know that you had to share a bed with your mother,' I said.

He gave an embarrassed laugh.

'No big deal,' I said.

'No big deal? She was my mother. How could I screw my own mother?' he said.

I stopped. What did he mean?

'When your mother caught you wanking, it must have been embarrassing,' I suggested.

'Yes.'

'So what happened?'

'She talked to me.'

'Just talked.'

'Yes, talked,' he shot me a nervous glance. 'What else would she do?'

'Tell me exactly what she said.'

'OK, she didn't say anything!' he shouted. 'She hit me.'

'Hit you?'

'Yes, hit.' He laughed suddenly. 'I'll tell you what happened. My mother said I was an animal, so she beat me like an animal. And she was right, I am an animal. You're human, aren't you? Swap places with me and we'll see. What if you woke up in the middle of the night, with no one there, only your mum. Only a mother. You might use your mum then.'

'What?'

'Sorry, I'm just talking rubbish.'

Now he was saying it. We always say we're talking rubbish when we're afraid the truth will come out.

'We've made our enquiries,' I said.

'About what?'

'You know.'

'What do I know?' he said. 'What?'

'The walls of your house are thin,' I said.

I'd struck home. He finally crumbled.

145

'I couldn't help it,' he began. 'She swore at me. She called it "that stuff". But what could I do? I had to do it. The worst time was waking up at three in the morning, when everything was dark. In the dark, you're trapped with your desires. Then the next day she swore at me and beat me. But I'm not a child any more. I hated her.'

'But why didn't she resist?'

'How do you know that?'

'You'd never have been able to beat her up, if she fought back. And she wouldn't have been left black and blue with bruises.'

'You can never prove it.'

'What?'

'That her body was bruised.'

'Of course we can,' I laughed. 'You only have to look at the autopsy.'

'You had no right to do that!' he shouted. 'She's my mum!'

He tried to stand up again, but swayed and fell. The guards went to heave him off the floor but he shoved them away. He started crawling out of the room, shouting 'Where's my mum? Where's my mum? You had no right to touch her! You had no right to do an autopsy!'

I ordered another autopsy.

They found traces of his semen in her vagina.

I burst into his cell and thrust the results at him. He scrunched the paper in his hand, as if afraid that others might see it. I tried to grab it off him, but he stuffed it in his mouth.

'It's no use,' I said. 'You can't hide it now.'

He went so still and limp he might have been dead.

'When?' I asked him.

'After she died,' he said. 'She'd left me. What was I to do?'

I looked him in the eye.

'It wasn't the first time,' I said.

'You don't know how difficult it was,' he said, 'when I woke up that night with a hard-on. I had to do it, even if Mum swore at me and hit me. I felt like I'd been stripped naked when she found out, I thought it was the end of everything. But then I realised that I never had to be ashamed again.

'After that I couldn't stop wanking. I did it over and over again, imagining fucking a girl, fucking her hole. But this was all fantasy. I'd never actually seen a woman's body. I had only ever seen my mum. Sometimes I caught a glimpse of a tit when she came out of the shower, or when we went to sleep.

'One night I saw a flash of her belly – one of the buttons on her top was undone and it was slightly open. I couldn't stop myself, I had to make my imaginings more real, so I adjusted the covers until I could see the lower part of one breast, a waning moon. I looked away and tried to get back to sleep.

'But the next night I had to have another look. This was a beautiful woman's body, right next to me. I'd seen the stupidest, ugliest women. But my mother – you've seen her. Even dead, she's stunning. Why would I choose someone ugly over her? It just doesn't make sense.'

'But this was your mother!'

'I borrowed her.' He smiled craftily. 'Just used her for a bit. Is that really so bad? And she wouldn't have got pregnant. Past that age. Maybe it sounds strange to you, but you can't understand famine until you're hungry.

'I heard about a shipwreck once. There was no sign of rescue and nothing left to eat or drink. Some of the survivors started to eat the corpses of their shipmates to stay alive. And why not? A dead man is made of meat, just like any animal. The only alternative was for everyone to starve while the flesh that could have saved their lives rotted around them.

'Here was a woman's body, here was a starving man, what was wrong with me using it?'

'What about morality?' I said.

He laughed grimly.

'There were two kinds of people on that boat: those who did what they had to, and those who became food for others. Which kind of person are you?'

'So she hit you?'

'Yes, she beat me,' he said. 'She pulled me upright and beat me, harder than ever before. I held on to her like a drowning man clings to a lifebuoy. I held my mother, and cried and cried. I was sorry that time.'

Beating him must have been like beating herself. Still, no one can beat themselves to death, any more than you can grab your own hair and pull yourself up off the ground.

'Then how did she die?' I said.

He answered without hesitation.

'I beat her to death. She made me hit her,' he went on. 'She said I had to beat her to death so she could forget everything.'

'But surely you knew your mother didn't want to die?'

A stupid question, of course. Nobody wants to die. But he clearly felt terrible about what he'd done. I was starting to feel sorry for him.

'Was it an accident?' I was trying to offer him a way out.

'No.'

Maybe he wanted to follow his mother but didn't have the courage to take his own life. Maybe he wanted us to do it for him. But I couldn't go along with that.

'Where did that whip come from?'

'My mum bought it.'

'When you bought the whip, did it have that sheath?'

'No, my mum made it later,' he answered. 'It took her a long time to find the right material.'

'So she did love you,' I said to him. 'You loved her too. Right?'

He didn't answer.

3. The Confession

Most crooks lie to the cops, I suppose, but not me. Even if the law lets me off the hook, it won't make any difference. I'm a prisoner of my body, and that's a life sentence.

People will forgive terrible crimes so long as you repent, because they find those same crimes in their own hearts. They're afraid, and forgiveness allows them to avoid confronting their fears.

Here I am, sitting in the interrogation room, the policeman looking at me, pen in hand, all ready to write down anything I say. You gave me a hint: 'We'll go easier on you'. I could take the hint, say I'd killed her by accident. That's what you want me to do. I could find an excuse, blame it on the system, on society. I know you're on my side, that you want to forgive my rebellion. But I wasn't rebelling. Rebelling doesn't solve anything, even if it feels good at the time. You might as well try to wash away cancer with a bath.

Chen Xiwo

The night the cops brought me home, I woke up in the middle of the night, sobbing. Mum held me in her arms and stroked my face. She wasn't wearing much, just thin pyjamas, and I could smell her armpits. When I was small, Mum was always sweaty. She would lift her top to give me milk from her sweaty breasts. That night I wanted to suck from her breasts again.

'Mum,' I said. 'I want to drink your milk.' I nuzzled her like a piglet.

'Silly boy,' she laughed. 'Drinking your mother's milk at your age? You should be ashamed of yourself.'

'I'm serious,' I said.

'That's enough.' She pulled away from me. 'I know you're really upset but just go to sleep. Tomorrow I'll start trying to find you a wife again.'

But I didn't want to marry another girl. I didn't dare look at my Mum any more.

The following evening, I clambered on to the bed and lay on my side. I could see her shadow chasing mosquitos through the net. The net billowed and her shadow moved with it. I shut my eyes.

When she got into bed I turned my back on her and shifted away. She quickly fell asleep, but I couldn't. I turned over and looked at her. She was lying with her back towards me. Her body was still young, still slim. She never had another child. She worked hard and didn't eat much. Her waist was so slender it looked like it might snap when she leaned forwards. You wanted to reach out and touch it.

I held back. I touched myself instead, and waited to see if her pyjamas would come open again. But that night her buttons were done up tight. I had to use my imagination

150

to bring myself off. The next day I was afraid Mum would find out what I'd done. But she didn't seem to notice. And my pyjama bottoms dried off.

The next night, I did it again. And the third and the fourth. But it wasn't enough. I moved closer to her body, bumped against it. It shrank away slightly. But she didn't wake. I leaned closer. Mum slept on. I put my leg on her body. I was dizzy with pleasure. Still, she didn't wake. How could she be in such a deep sleep?

I came on her body, crying out 'Mum.'

The body stirred slightly. But she slept on. It was as if she was dead. I actually hoped that she was dead. Now that I was satisfied, I could die too.

Very gently, I wiped my come from Mum's body.

The next morning she got up as if nothing happened, though that morning she took a shower and changed her clothes. But she changed her top too, and I hadn't got anything on that. Maybe she hadn't noticed. She cooked up some rice, brought it to me, told me to start eating and started clearing up.

'Mum,' I said, 'do the washing up when we've finished eating.'

She didn't answer.

'Mum!' I shouted.

'Don't call me Mum!' she screeched.

Of course she knew. I was stupid to have hoped she didn't.

But I'd always called her Mum. Maybe I'd always had those feelings for her too. She was the most beautiful woman in the world to me. Once she took me to a department store and sat me on top of a counter to rest her back. One of the assistants shouted at her. She looked like a slut with her makeup, her ludicrous pencilled eyebrows. I didn't want a girl like that for my wife, I wanted my mum. I loved my mum.

A few days later, Mum said we should go for a walk. After carrying me for quite some distance she stopped at a massage parlour. Perhaps a massage might help, she suggested. The whole place was painted red, you could hardly see the women's faces for makeup but the flesh on show was clear enough. I knew what was going on straight away.

A girl led us into a cubicle smelling of stale perfume and cigarettes and men. Mum put me down on the massage table, gave the girl a look and said she was going shopping. I wasn't bothered about going to a prostitute. People do all sorts of things these days – husbands, fathers, workers, good citizens. Sex is just a physical thing. No big deal.

She put her hand on my cock. It was like lightning. Not that she wasn't gentle. She was very young, very young and very gentle. I only sat there, so she took off her clothes, just like that, to reveal a body that was the kind of body I'd been dreaming of.

My dick stood up like a rifle. Now I could be a soldier, I could throw myself into battle.

She slithered on top of me, moving softly, like a snake. She licked my nipples and took hold of me, to guide me in.

But was this what I really wanted?

I jerked violently. She fell off the narrow table.

'You really thought I'd do it with someone like you?' She sneered. 'If it wasn't for your mother … '

When my mum came to collect me she was really embarrassed. She went bright red and carried me out.

'What a dreadful place,' she said. 'I thought they'd do you

152

a proper massage.'

But all I wanted was to love, was to be loved. This was nothing to do with anyone else. My mum had been willing to give herself to that decrepit old man so I could get a wife, so why wouldn't she give herself to me? Mum would never deny me anything, she was the one who loved me most. And I was going to love her back.

That night she turned out the light, got into bed and lay still with her back towards me. I wanted to go inside, deep inside. She must have known what I wanted, but what could she do? As she pretended to be asleep, I took off her pyjama bottoms. She resisted a little, but she didn't turn over.

I was going to hell.

Straight to hell.

I entered her.

She quivered and stirred as if in her sleep, shifting position slightly. That made it easier for me. Everything was going fine. I even convinced myself that she'd given in. Maybe she was even pretending that I was another man. I could pretend she was another woman, but I didn't want to. This was the only woman I wanted.

I cried out 'Mum!'

She must have heard, but she didn't stir. I had to say it. I wanted this person, not a hole, not flesh. This was my mother.

So long as she kept her eyes shut she could pretend it wasn't happening. I was just using her, just using her once, that was all. No big deal. But my mother was a coward. She was determined not to wake up.

I couldn't hold on any longer.

I came.

The next morning I asked her if she slept well.

'Yes.' She looked dazed. 'I was very tired yesterday.'

'You mean even an earthquake wouldn't have woken you?'

A flicker of despair on her face.

'No. And if I die, then I die, and that's that.'

'What will I do if you die?'

'That's why I've got to find you a wife,' she said. She hadn't mentioned that for a while.

'An idiot,' I sneered.

She smiled sadly.

'I'll find you the best I can.'

'That's you,' I said.

'What rubbish. Eat up. As soon as you've finished I have to go out. I don't have time to talk rubbish.'

She left her clothes on the bed when she left, laid out top and bottom, like a person. My mother. I threw myself on them, touched them, sniffed them. I wrapped them around me and brought myself off again.

When she came back she tidied them all away, as if nothing had happened. I called her over.

'Come here a minute, Mum.'

'Why?'

'I need to piss.'

She brought over the chamber pot and put it at my feet. I leaned on her while she helped me off the bed and undid my trousers.

I put my arms around her. We were face to face in broad daylight.

'Why don't you just go to sleep?' she said and pushed me away.

I fell to the ground. I couldn't get up – I'm a cripple – so she helped me. Mum had to hold on to me.

I held her again.

She lashed out at me, then slipped and fell. I slid to the ground next to her. She cried out, then crawled over and propped me up once more. We sat on the ground, breathing heavily, like two dogs after a fight. She didn't dare look at me.

She smacked the floor.

'Why do you want it to be like this!'

'Mum, I love you!'

'Rubbish.'

'Mum, do you love me?'

'Yes,' she said. 'But that's different. I'm sorry. It's my fault you're crippled. I can make it up to you. I'll find you a good wife. A really good one. You believe your mum.'

'So what's a good wife?'

'One who's honest and beautiful.' Her face lit up. 'A wife who is one hundred percent good.'

'But you're the only one who can look after me, Mum.'

'No!' she said. 'Anyway, you don't treat me like your mother.'

'If you're not my mother, then what's the problem?'

'You're treating me like a bad mother,' she said.

'So you can do anything.'

'I don't want to.'

'Don't you love me, Mum?'

'No.'

'Really?'

'Don't make me,' Mum said. 'I don't want to go to hell … '

She stared at me with blank, terrified eyes.

'Hit me,' she said. 'I don't want to live. Beat me to death.'

She grabbed my hand and hit herself with it. I tried to stop

155

her, but she was so strong. She gripped me so tight I cried out with pain. She stopped and rubbed my hand to make it better. Then she burst into tears.

'I'm not a good mum. Hit me! Hit me! Hit me!'

We both wept.

A bit later she said she could bring me off with her hand. She wasn't ashamed, she was just embarrassed. I said no.

'Do you think I wanted you to do that to me? Do you?' she shouted, hurling a plate to the floor. She cut her finger on the shards and I took her hand. It was so thin. I told her she could bring me off with it.

Mum washed her hands and put antiseptic on her finger, then stopped. It wasn't like undressing me for a bath. This was different.

She poked my cock with her finger. It lengthened.

It felt amazing. She just lifted up my prick, just like when I was a naughty boy and she would pat me on the cheek, more of a caress than a smack. Like a mother. She lifted it with her finger. The antiseptic looked like blood.

Just the two of us. Outside the murmur of traffic and the shouts of the market traders, as if from far away. I came. She pressed her finger to the end and gave my prick a shake, to make the come flow back. Then she wiped the tip, like she was mopping the last drop of sauce from the pan. We never wasted leftovers. What we had, we looked after.

When she was washing her hands I caught sight of her round arse. I wanted it. Her hand wasn't good enough. Her fingers didn't make a real hole.

'Mum, next time use your mouth.'

She looked at me like I was a monster.

'No! How could you imagine such a thing? You're getting

worse and worse.'

'It's just another hole, Mum.'

'Don't call me that,' she yelped. 'Look what you've made me into.'

'Just once.'

'Not even once.'

I started to moan. She tried to ignore me, but then she ran out of the room. I sat there, rocking backwards and forwards like I was going to explode.

'Mum!' I cried.

She said nothing. I wanked until I thought my cock would come off. I cried out in pain. She rushed back into the room.

'What are you doing?' she shouted. 'The penis is the root of life. You'll kill yourself.'

'I have to.' I was weeping.

'If you want to die, kill me first. Kill me first. Kill me!'

She grabbed my hand again, hit me and then started to hit herself with my hand. I didn't resist. I was full of hate. We hit together. I hit her until we were both exhausted.

'OK,' she said.

I looked down and saw I wasn't hard any more.

'If you can't bear it, then just hit me,' she said.

'No,' I said. 'I won't hit you.'

But I wanted to. She brought out a leather whip. Where had that come from?

'Use this,' she said.

'I won't hit you,' I said.

'I'm telling you, do it!' she yelled.

I took the whip.

'I'm a bad mother,' she said.

'No, no, I won't.'

'Do it!' she said. She grabbed my hand and thwacked the whip on her body. Cool air rushed across my face. She cried out.

'Does it hurt?' I asked.

'No, it's good,' she said. The second blow came from me.

'That hurts,' she said.

'What?'

'You didn't hit so hard,' she explained. 'That really hurts.' I did it again.

'Silly boy,' she said. 'Are you trying to make me suffer?' I hit her hard. Mum gave a shrill cry.

'You're such a bad boy.' She was trying to talk to me as if everything was normal. As long as she was calling me a good boy or a bad boy, we could do anything we wanted.

'Mum, I want to stand up to hit you,' I said.

She lay down and braced me upright against her raised arm, like I was really standing, like I was a normal person. I hit her again.

Soon the pain made her let go and I collapsed in a heap. She pushed me back up again and lay on the floor.

'Mum, get up, give me something to aim at.'

She stood and put her arms around me. I couldn't use the whip, because we were too close together, but if she moved away I couldn't stand up.

'Mum, let me ride on your back.'

She lay on her stomach, but I kept missing and dropped the whip. She crawled over to get it and gave it back to me.

'What's wrong with your hand?' she asked.

'Just a bit of broken skin, it's nothing.'

She examined the whip handle.

'Where was this made?' she said. 'So rough. Nothing is

well made these days.'

She bandaged up my hand and made a sheath for the handle out of some old rags. You could hardly see the seam. The cotton was so soft on my hand. It made me want to cry.

'Do you really want this, Mum?'

'Yes, I really do,' she said.

'Does it feel good?'

'Yes.'

'You're just saying it.'

'Silly child!' Mum said. 'If it's good for you, then it's good for me.'

'I can make you feel good, Mum.' I pulled at her arm. 'I want to do it with you again.'

'Get off me!' she shouted, furious.

'You don't love me anymore.'

'I do.'

'It's not true. You hate me. You'd be so much happier without me.'

'And you hate me as well, you useless creature.'

'Yes!' I said.

'So hit me, you vicious boy!'

And I did.

'Again.'

I wanted to kill her. She would rather have my hate than my love. She groaned. I groaned as well. My whip was very hard.

She cried out once, but she didn't want to waste her breath. She held it in like a jug holds the smell of a good wine. With every blow her ecstasy increased. She was so far gone she couldn't move. How could she think only of her own pleasure? I had to wake her up.

159

Chen Xiwo

But how?

I knew. I knew what she was most afraid of. As I fucked her I shouted 'Mum, Mum! I love you, I love you, Mum! I love you, Mum!'

Write that down. Make sure you write that down. You're looking at me as if I'm despicable, as if I deserve to die, as if my dead body should be paraded through the streets. You think I'm some kind of animal, but look around you. We're all animals. You won't admit it, I know. You've been washed clean of your mother's blood. You're civilised. You have a clear conscience …

In 1877, Lewis H Morgan in his work Ancient Society observed that American Iroquois Indians have a very unusual naming convention for kinsfolk. They address their biological father as 'Father', but also all of their father's brothers. In the same way, 'my mother's sister is my mother'. This form of address is like a living fossil that preserves information about primitive bloodlines. Similarly in Chinese, the word 姐 (jie) originally meant 'mother', as shown in a number of old works, and yet in common speech today the word is used to mean 'wife', 'lover' or 'young woman'. 娘 (niang) means 'mother', but the original meaning was 'young woman'. An ancient dictionary says: 'Niang: a word meaning young girl'. The Southern Dynasties poem 'Midnight Songs' has this lyric: 'See a beautiful young girl's happy face/ she hopes to make a golden match.' But the word used here for 'young girl" 娘子 (niangzi) also meant 'wife.'

Are you sure about this?
You can shut the book now.
Do you choose to read on?

Going to Heaven

1

When I was learning to write, I always got a thrill as I traced over the character 'death' in my red-lined copybook. Some Chinese characters are so expressive: the character 'smile', 笑, looks like a radiant grin, and 'cry', 哭, has a sad face. 'Death', 死, looks like someone meeting the end fearlessly, head on.

My dad used to make his living from the dead. He was an undertaker. Our house was always filled with strangers coming and going. My dad would paste up hand-written leaflets with his address and phone number in the towns and villages nearby: 'For all weddings and funerals – you're in safe hands with us.' Eventually he began to get his notices printed and they looked as elegant as wedding invitations.

My dad was a fine figure of a man with big square features and ruddy cheeks like Lord Guan, the legendary general in The Romance of the Three Kingdoms. My grandmother used to sigh 'With a face like that, you should have been a civil servant, but you ended up messing about with ghosts.' I never understood what my granny had against my dad's line of business.

Dad always kept things very relaxed in the office, handing out cigarettes to the bereaved. They hardly ever tried to bargain him down – when they thought the price was too high, they simply found some excuse to leave. If anyone did have the nerve to start bargaining, my dad would draw himself up to his full height, and say: 'Are you trying to get this thing done properly, or just save money?'

And they would fall silent.

My father always refused to haggle because it would demean his profession. And the truth was, hardly anyone tried to scrimp and save where a burial was concerned. You might be poor in life, but never in death. My dad took their money and put it to good use – he was a good businessman. He only ever carried a battered leather briefcase packed with pens, notebooks and rope, but once the family bought him paper and cloth, he could fit out a mourning room with flowers, swags and hangings in no time at all. If he made them buy a lot, they thought he'd done a good job – he wasn't worried about taking their money.

When someone died, crowds of mourners would show up and stand around chatting. Gifts of carpets and bedding to honour the deceased were piled against the walls, with heaps of silver candles and coloured cakes all over the floor. Everyone talked and laughed and waited for the food, as if they'd come to a party. It was a chance for people who had not met in years to meet up. They gave out name cards and talked about how to stay in touch. Even before the burial, people would be fixing up drinking competitions for the wake and laying bets that they could drink each other under the table.

Going to Heaven

When my dad had a funeral to arrange my mum helped too, so I got taken along. I enjoyed mooching around the mourning room. Even when I was pretty small, I was quite used to it all – the smell, the casket with the dead person. The first time I saw one, I thought it looked funny.

'What's that?' I asked.

'A coffin,' said the grown-ups. Or, at least, that's what I realised later. At the time, I thought they said 'coffer' – somewhere for a rich man to keep his savings. No wonder a funeral was a big show like a wedding.

The coffin was always a gleaming red. I could never understand why it was such a cheerful colour when someone had died, but red was for a big occasion. When someone died the neighbours had to let the family put tables burning incense outside the door, and had to put up with the noise of fire crackers, the smoke and smell of candles and paper offerings, the general pandemonium. No one could complain, because there had been a death.

The music started up at first light. I loved the tunes, I loved listening to the trumpets and tubas. The players all dressed up in military uniforms with badges and peaked caps. Sometimes, if we went to a crematorium, other families would have their own musicians, dressed in different uniforms. Each funeral had its own band with outfits in all colours – green, blue and red – and as soon as one finished playing, another took over.

Our bandleader was a man with one eye. He could play anything. When he first arrived, he had his tuba tied to his back with a piece of rope.

'What can you play, One Eye?' asked my dad.

'Anything. I only have to hear it once on TV.'

'I don't want any old thing from the TV,' said my dad sternly. 'I'll tell you just want I want: Serving as a Soldier.'

So One Eye stretched out his neck like a cockerel and started to play Serving as a Soldier. He followed up with Where is Happiness?, A Springtime Story, Into New Times, and The Wedding Sedan ... 'taking my bride in my arms into the wedding sedan'. He really could play anything.

As he tootled away on his tuba, Dad laughed and said: 'OK, One Eye, god may have messed up your eye, but at least you've got a good mouth on you. You certainly can play a good tune.'

One Eye never had any money. He was no good at farming and he was no businessman. He couldn't afford a wife, so he spent all day playing his tuba and took it to bed with him at night. Before he started in our band, he had so little to eat, he was half starved. Luckily for him there were always weddings and funerals.

Dad looked down on One Eye, and didn't try to hide it. One Eye wore his band uniform all the time – it was his best outfit. 'That's for when you're in the band!' Dad shouted at him. 'If you wear it out, you'll have to buy a new one.'

One Eye was the leader of the band, always the first to play, making splurting sounds as the tip of his tongue licked away at the tuba. As soon as he started to play, the other band members joined in, making a great wave of sound. Then One Eye would stop, take his lips from the tuba, swear at this musician for losing his way or that one for playing out of tune, and carry on.

Everyone liked his the way he played, but if they asked him for a solo, he always refused. The most he would do was a bit of spluttering with his tongue, not making any sound, just to tease the audience. 'Don't keep us waiting, One Eye,' they shouted. 'It's like you're going down on a woman and then not screwing her.'

There was always a big crowd around the band, humming along to the tune while the bereaved family went around offering tea and welcoming the guests. But they weren't perfect. For instance, they always dragged out the notes of Hold Me In Your Arms, which kept you in suspense, as if you were about to step out into the void. And when they had to get up and lead the procession for the coffin it was mayhem – there was no way the pallbearers could keep in step behind. Luckily the funeral was usually such chaos by then that no one noticed.

There was lots to look out for before the procession set off. First the coffin was turned around, the head of the coffin raised up, and my father began the service. The chief mourners bowed low, my father read out the rites and the sons and daughters walked three times round the coffin. The coffin was nailed shut with plenty of nails – to symbolise the dead man's descendants, my dad told me. Then the coffin was lifted up again and they were off, the eldest son leading the way holding the funeral banner and the second son walking behind, cradling a board with the name of the departed. Other family members followed on with white-wrapped mourning staffs, the oldest daughter-in-law carrying a pot full of delicious food to be buried at the head of the coffin, so that the departed had something to good to eat. The relatives in the procession were a patchwork of different colours: light yellow, dark yellow, red and white. The band members never wanted to leave, and just stood there gawping.

My dad was always furious: 'What are you doing still

hanging around? Are you a bunch of stiffs?'

He always called them stiffs when they were standing around. He yelled at them when they were busy too, busy eating that is. The banquet after the funeral was the part they looked forward to the most – they would head back to the house, sit down at a table and tuck in. Whenever we got new musicians, they were always skinny as monkeys, but gradually they filled out. Every time a main dish came into the room they had to stand up and play it in. They'd get up slowly, still eating, snatching mouthfuls between notes. 'How can you play with your mouths full of food,' my dad would shout. 'You'll choke!'

Dad was never greedy and always full of energy. He was the boss. When he did a reading, people shouted 'Bravo!' The band would strike up and play another tune, then Dad would do another reading – they were always appropriate to the deceased. If it was an old man he would read:

'Take your time, old man,
We will see you to the door.
Your relatives and friends will see you on your way,
They'll drink themselves under the table for you.'

'Bravo!'

'Go in peace, old man,
Go where you will.
Keep on spending your money,
Get that pork knuckle on to cook.'

'Bravo!'

'Go without a care,
Your sons and grandsons are all scholars.
Each generation is stronger than the last,
They have power, they have wealth.'

'Bravo!'

'Laugh and be happy, old man,
You've left the family in good hands.
When they piss into the bottle,
They don't spill a drop.'

'Bravo!'

Everyone always loved it. They drank, they toasted the departed, they talked, and drank, and drank again, and talked, and made a tremendous racket.

2

But good times never last. Once everyone had eaten their fill and picked their teeth, they gathered up the gifts from their hosts and staggered off, like a noisy crowd heading home after a film. Dad lit the hell money and the flames consumed the colourful bank notes. I wanted to hang around, but it was time for me to go, time to go and not come back. The first time I asked the host 'When are we coming back again?' he was appalled.

'Stupid kid!' shouted my dad, and clouted me.

All the grown-ups said I was stupid. I couldn't understand why. Why was the host so grumpy just because someone had died? It didn't make any sense. Whenever grown-ups talked about death, they just kept repeating the same things.

After the service was over, there was a week of offerings to the spirit of the departed. This was called 'doing the sevens'. The sevens were fun – the best part was burning paper houses. They were made from strips of bamboo, tied together with string and pasted all over with paper. The houses were magnificent, big and bright, nicer than the real houses the families lived in. There were courtyards in front and gardens behind. There were beds and furniture, TVs and music systems. And there were maids. The painter would wet his brush with spit and dip it in the paints. He'd draw two fat bulges on their fronts and give me a multi-coloured, paint-besmeared grin. Once he gave one of the servants a big bulge in its crotch. I didn't understand.

'Boy servant,' said the painter.

I still didn't understand. It was a woman who died, the painter explained with a smile. I half-understood, and smiled back.

Then he drew something else. 'What's that?' I asked.

'A mobile.'

'A mobile?' I'd heard of those.

'You can do all sorts of things with a mobile,' the painter said.

While we were making the paper house outside, the Daoist priest was reciting prayers inside the house with his eyes clos¬ed. The priest summoned the immortals, drawing them in with delicate eddies of incense. Crowded into the memorial hall, they ate and drank their fill. The priest was a superman. No one was really scared of my dad but they were all scared of the priest. He was paraplegic.

He had been handsome when he was young, so they said, an all-round good-looker, though a little short. So when he heard about a machine that could make him taller, he decided to buy one with the money he had put aside to get a wife – he reckoned he'd have no trouble getting married once he was bigger. 'Who wants to live with a deformity?' he said, 'I'd be better off dead.'

The machine made him taller all right, but after a year it had weakened the muscles in his back so much he couldn't straighten up when he walked – it was too painful. Sweating with fear, he scuttled off to see a doctor, who said the machine had strained his spinal cord. He was lucky to be able to stand up and walk at all, even with a hump. He spent days crying and moaning in despair, until he was completely exhausted. It was too much to bear. He wasn't even as tall as he had been before. He tried to kill himself, but his friends stopped him. At least he could still walk, they said, it was just that his back was a bit painful, that was all.

Eventually, he became paralysed.

His friends took every knife, every piece of rope, every medicine bottle out of his reach so he couldn't kill himself. He had to go on living in agony. He used to ask for a massage, for people to press, knead, beat or stand on his back while he cried out in anguish as if he was being tortured. But after it was over he relaxed, bliss written all over his face. 'That's better,' he said. 'Life is good!'

For him, it was bliss to be numb, to feel no pain. I realised later that people often live with pain. Happiness is just the lack of pain, health the absence of an aching belly or creaking joints. As soon as you start to feel something, you're ill.

Eventually he went through the wall, like the masters of Mount Lao, and crossed into another realm. He made contact with the worlds of both yin and yang – and became a Daoist priest.

Dad used to say he wasn't like us. He was a man who had seen the king of the underworld, a man with one foot in the land of the living and the other in the land of the dead – not that his feet were much use. His body was such a mess that it was hard to imagine the handsome young man he had been. But his eyes were still bright, as if all his energy was focused in them. My dad said those eyes could see things that were invisible to ordinary folk. He always had the greatest respect for the priest, though he despised everyone else. That was too bad for One Eye – no one could make him paralysed, like the priest.

My dad always asked the priest to do the funeral ceremonies. He couldn't use his legs, so someone had to carry him into the suffocating darkness of the dead person's house. Some boy would prop the door open, another would shift things out of the way. There was a great commotion. One Eye would start to shout: 'Get back! Get back! Make way for the priest!' But the priest took no notice. He heard nothing, he saw nothing. With his body limp and his eyes closed he might have been half dead, but he still had enormous presence. In fact his presence came from being half dead – that was why he became a priest in the first place, why everyone was afraid of him.

At one funeral, I did something pretty stupid. A young

woman had died but we didn't go to her house, we went to the government buildings in the local capital. I was scared. Normally we'd keep well away from the gate in case the police arrested us, but the family weren't worried. They laid the dead body down by the entrance.

My dad wasn't worried either – he set the memorial room up right there. The white cloth was covered with black characters I couldn't read and the grown-ups said the writing was an accusation against a senior official who worked there.

'Which one?' I asked.

'A head of department. You wouldn't understand.'

What did they mean, I wouldn't understand? Eventually I picked up that the official wanted to sleep with the young woman and she refused, so he got her drunk and dragged her off to his hotel room. When she woke up and realised what had happened, she ran away and threw herself in the river.

Candles flickered round the dead girl and the hell money burned, filling the air with confetti. The charred paper settled on the sentries' peaked caps. They didn't look scary, just bored – they couldn't be bothered to flick it off. The family glared at the gate and yelled, their arms akimbo, or clutched the body, weeping and wailing into a loudspeaker that shook the building to the foundations. After they had cried themselves hoarse, my dad told the funeral band to start playing. He was as caught up in the funeral as the family. So were all the bystanders. They looked really pissed off.

Finally the manager came out of the building. No one knew who he was and they all demanded to see the city's chief executive. The manager said that was impossible. I wasn't surprised. Why would the city chief want to see ordinary people like us? I didn't even know what he looked like. But the crowd wouldn't let it go.

'We can sort this out,' said the manager. 'Why are you all making such a fuss?'

'We've waited for ages! The only reason you came out was because we're making a fuss.'

'But this is against the law.'

'Against the law?' they shouted back. 'You've got nerve to talk about the law!'

The manager was furious. He pulled out a mobile and called the police. I was pretty scared by then, and couldn't understand why nobody else was. But they didn't back down. The police came and tried to push them out of the way, but they pushed back. A couple of people got arrested, but the others ran to the body and clung on tight. The inspector was livid. 'Take that corpse away!' he shouted. His officers tried to drag the family off, but they stuck to it like limpets. People shouted: 'The police are stealing the body!'

'Hands off!' My dad's voice rang out. 'Or there will be vengeance.'

The policemen froze.

'Aren't you afraid she'll come after you?' Dad said darkly. 'Female spirits are dangerous!'

The police let go and took a step back, waiting to see what the inspector would say. Then the family started attacking the police with their fists. 'Does nobody ever die in your family?' they yelled. 'What if your sister was raped too!' The police began to back off, step by step. It was amazing – I couldn't believe it – they were useless. I wanted to beat them up too. How stupid to be scared of these paper tigers – they stood with the living and we stood with the dead.

When you're dead you have nothing more to fear. You

become invincible, like the dead girl. That's why we make offerings to our ancestors, so they don't turn into ghosts and come and get us. That's why dying is such a powerful thing. The only reason you have no power is because you're not dead yet, because you're afraid of dying. Sure it's painful – that girl must have suffered a lot – but she made it through and now she is a spirit.

In the end, the city chief agreed to see the girl's family. They didn't look at all afraid as they went in, as if the girl's spirit was hovering over them like a threat. My dad told my mum that the mayor was worried about publicity, that the county had set targets for the number of unnatural deaths each year. If they didn't meet the target, the county leader would lose his job. 'This is a dreadful case,' Dad said, though he sounded pretty pleased. At least the girl's death had got her family in to see the chief.

'We can't take the corpse for cremation yet,' Dad added. 'We have to keep it. Once it's cremated, it's useless.'

3

The head of department got the sack and the family got a big payout, so the sevens got a bit rowdy. But there seemed to be something bothering the Daoist priest as he conducted the ceremonies. While he was reciting the prayers, his long, black lashes flickered – he kept taking sneaky glances at her picture. She was very pretty.

During one of the breaks, I found myself alone with the priest – the family was busy outside and the monks had gone for a drink of water.

'She was pretty, wasn't she?' he said.

I nodded.

'That's why he went for her. In this world, there's always a price to be paid if you're good-looking. It's better to be plain. If you're good-looking you have to be born lucky too. Otherwise evil will be done. Do you see?'

I half-understood … Suddenly the priest said: 'She's smiling.'

I jumped and looked at the body. It was true, the girl was smiling.

'If you're born unlucky, you'll only find peace in death,' the priest went on. 'It's too bad. That's one less woman to get married.'

I had no idea what he meant. He mumbled something – it was as if he was speaking from inside an urn.

'What?'

'Shh!' he held his finger to his lips. Then suddenly he came out with: 'Why don't I give her to you?'

'To me?'

'To marry. Do you know what marriage means?'

Of course I knew. People who were very close got married. I wanted to marry my friend Blockhead once, but he didn't want to. He wanted to marry his sister.

The priest chuckled. 'You don't understand a thing.'

'I do!' I said.

'OK, OK, you do,' he agreed. 'So, if you're going to marry her, you have to step over the coffin.'

'Step over the coffin?'

'The husband has to step over the wife's coffin. Then she's yours.'

Mine. I really wanted a sister. Once I asked my mum why she only had me, but she said it was because of Dad: 'You can never tell what's going to happen, he'd say, best not to have another.' So I never got a big sister like Blockhead's. His sister used to carry him around when he was little. I used to see him riding on her back, legs sticking out either side, and wonder why he didn't get pins and needles.

I nodded.

'Once you're married, will you be good to her?'

'Yes!'

'How?'

I was stumped. I'd only ever thought of what older sisters could do for their younger brothers. This girl was laid out flat, so how could she do anything for me? But I really wanted a big sister, so I turned it all around: I'd do things for her. 'I'll carry her on my back.' I said.

'What else?'

'I'll give her nice food.'

'What else?'

'And ...' I suddenly remembered that my mum was always complaining that she hadn't had a daughter to help around the house. 'I'll help her round the house.'

'Help her with what?' the priest asked with a smile.

I smiled too.

'So you haven't thought about sleeping with her?' he asked.

Oh, of course. My mum was always saying I was going to fall out of bed when I was asleep. If I had a big sister, she'd stop me rolling off. And if I kicked off the covers, a big sister would tuck me in. 'I'll tuck her in,' I said.

'Just tuck her in?' the priest said. 'Nothing else?'

What else was there? I couldn't think of anything. A smile glinted in his eyes. He was trying to trap me, so I stopped talking and wandered over to the paper house. The painter had built something different this time: a big, tall building.

'It's a skyscraper,' the painter said. 'They've got buildings like that overseas. Young people nowadays all want to live in places like these. That's why that poor kid came to the city. The skyscrapers are in the city.'

He meant the girl, I knew that.

'And now you've got your own skyscraper to live in,' the painter muttered. 'It's not even rented, it's yours. We're giving you a big, tall skyscraper and a passport too, and you can move to America.'

'What's a passport?' I asked.

'You can go abroad with it,' said the painter.

'Go abroad where?'

The painter beamed. 'To Sky-land.'

'Sky-land?'

'That's heaven, another world. The priest will be sending the girl there soon, it's a good place.'

'I want to go too.'

'You can't go,' said the painter. 'It's like a pane of glass. You can see through, but something stops you when you reach out. You can't go there.'

The painter raised his hand as if he wanted to touch the sky but couldn't – just like there really was a pane of glass over our heads.

'So how do this house and the things in it get through?' I asked.

'They can get through when we burn them.'

I always felt it was a waste to burn the paper houses. But if you didn't burn them, they wouldn't go to heaven. It didn't matter how pretty the girl's skyscraper was, it had to burn.

The monks stood around the fire with the family and their guests, their faces sinister, their eyes gleaming in the light of the flickering flames. Four fierce men came in, carrying the swaying skyscraper on a pair of poles. They hurled it on to the fire with a great heave and wiped the dust from their hands. Tongues of flame licked at cardboard treasure chests, packed with fake gold ingots, blackening them and turning them to ash. One after another, they threw everything on to the blaze.

That's when I did something really stupid. A man came in, pouring with sweat. He was holding something in his hand. As he brushed past me, I saw it was a mobile phone – a real mobile phone, not a paper one.

We didn't have a mobile. Even if we got one, my dad would never let me play with it. If I could just get hold of this one, maybe I could sneak it outside and play with it. I wanted to take a look at it, but the man raised his arm. What was he going to do with it? No surely not, I couldn't let him. I threw myself at him to snatch the phone from his hand. People shouted: 'What's that kid doing?'

But I was too late. The man had launched it over-arm and the phone was already in the flames. I rushed forward to pull it out but something, or someone, was holding me back. People were shrieking. Someone was grabbing me and I struggled. I wanted that mobile. The flames crackled and the phone began to burn, but I struggled harder than ever, with a strength I didn't know I had. For a moment I was free, but then they held me down and shouted for my dad.

I couldn't care less, I almost had that phone. Then my dad appeared out of nowhere and shoved me away from the fire.

By the time I looked around again, the phone had vanished. I burst into tears.

I never dared cry in front of my dad, not even when he beat me. Crying was defiance, he said. But I cried now. I didn't care what he did. My mobile had gone to heaven. It belonged to my big sister, and to me too, but I couldn't reach it. It flew higher and higher, leaving nothing but wisps of smoke behind in this world. Behind the curtain of flames, the monks on the other side of the fire seemed to tremble, like cicada wings. Their shapes were distorted too, as if they were made of running water, their chanting muffled as if it was coming from the depths of a river. Only the clashing of the cymbals was clear, that and the mouth of the Daoist priest as he carried on praying.

As the fire grew fiercer and the smoke cleared, the flames leaped on to the house of the bereaved family. All the grown-ups panicked and started to fight the blaze. All except the priest. He stood motionless, reciting in the loudest voice I had ever heard. The girl's mother cried out: 'It's burning! It's all going to burn down!' And the Daoist raised his voice again, like a demon urging the fire to burn more brightly until it consumed the whole vile world. He seemed to merge with the flames, his voice a powerful beam of magical light, which rose up to the skies like a ladder reaching right to the threshold of heaven:

'Sister rise to heaven.
We send you on a journey,
We send you to the first layer of heaven.

This is the middle heaven.
We send you to the second layer of heaven,
Above the middle heaven.
At the third layer of heaven,
The immortals dance.
The immortals come to meet you.
You go to the fourth layer of heaven.
The fifth layer is bright heaven,
The sixth layer is spacious heaven,
Here is boundless beauty.
The seventh layer is harmonious heaven,
The eighth layer is limitless depths,
The ninth layer of heaven is perfection.
In heaven there is no rape.'

4

I got sick. I lay in bed with a fever while mum stroked my
forehead, asking 'Do you want something to eat?'

I didn't want anything to eat. I wanted a mobile. I don't
know why I needed it so badly. Maybe I wanted it all the
more because it wasn't there to have. It had already gone up
to the ninth heaven where it was far out of my reach. Only
big sister at the heavenly gates could have it. I dreamed of
them swinging wide to let her in with her red gown, tucking
her red parasol under her arm. I so wanted to go with her. I
dreamed of her playing with the phone. I was beside myself.

Even if I asked her for it, she wouldn't give it to me. It was hers, not mine. If I had it, I wouldn't give it up.

'Mum,' I said. 'I want a mobile.'

'A mobile?'

'A mobile phone.'

'Really?' she said. 'I'll ask your dad.'

I wouldn't normally want Mum to ask Dad, because he'd really tell me off. But this time I wasn't scared.

Dad came home cursing and swearing, saying the family's house had burnt down. It wasn't his fault, he said, it was the mother who set it on fire while she was cooking. But the funeral hadn't been a success, and he always wanted everything to go well. Dad said it was all because I'd made a fuss. He didn't know what had got into me. I must have gone mad. And what kind of a job was being an undertaker anyway, if it sent his son crazy.

Mum told Dad I wanted a mobile. Dad was furious: 'I haven't even started with you yet, and you've got the cheek to start asking for presents!'

Mum pulled Dad to one side and started whispering. Dad sighed and his tone softened. 'Not even city folks can afford a mobile,' he told me. 'That girl probably wanted one her whole life and didn't get one. I suppose the family bought her a fake one, with that big payout.'

'I want a fake one!' I said.

Dad got furious again. 'If you want a fake one, then you'll have to go to heaven.'

'I want to go to heaven!'

Mum butted in: 'Stupid child. Don't say things like that.'

I really did want to go to heaven, but to do that I had to die like big sister. Dying sounded painful. The least painful way would probably be starvation, I thought, to lie in bed all day, not eating a thing, your strength ebbing away until you died. So I said I felt bloated and went without a few meals. After a while, I started to feel weaker, so I held my breath for a test. It felt like the air had been sucked out of me and I was floating away, like I could float all the way to the ninth heaven. But I couldn't hold my breath forever. I let it out – my body felt like it was weighed down with lead.

Trying to make myself die was too difficult, like trying to take off into the sky by pulling on my own hair. I needed some help, but I couldn't get that at home, I had to go elsewhere. But going out needed strength. I needed to eat. Mum did me noodles and I gulped them down. I hated the way they were mixed with all sorts of things like meat and clams that bumped against the edge of the bowl and got in the way. Mum said I liked clams but I didn't like them any more. I'd stopped liking anything on earth. I was already on my way to heaven.

I finished my dinner and was just about to go out when Dad came back. He didn't like me going out to play. 'Why do kids want to play outside for?' he always said. He sat down for a smoke in the hall, right in my way. He looked as if he was going to be there forever. I watched his cigarette glowing in the gloom. I was burning up like the shreds of his tobacco. Why didn't he have an appointment? Were people worried about the fire at the girl's house? He finished his cigarette and my heart skipped a beat. But he got out another one, tapped it with his finger and lit up again. Would he ever finish? He smoked one cigarette after another. I started hoping he'd finish the whole pack, so he'd send me out to get some more. At least I'd get out of the house.

Finally he stood up and went into his room. In a flash, I was out of the door. I only wanted to get away. By the time he found me I'd be dead – he couldn't beat me then.

Big sister drowned in the river, so that's where I went. There was no one by the water apart from a goggle-eyed frog. It could see me with its big eyes, but it had no idea who I was or what I was doing. Stupid frog. I didn't want it watching me anyway, I didn't want it to see the excitement on my face. So I chased it away.

Now nothing could stop me. Nobody would know what I was doing until it was done. Success. What a thought. It really did seem like death was a success. When everyone said someone had succeeded, it was because they had a good job, or got a lot of money, or did well in their exams or made a lot of friends. For me, success was death. I wanted to be a spirit. To succeed like that, I really had to watch out. Some fairy might be hiding in the grass, spying on me. River crabs were scuttling around on the bank. There were the fish too, swimming back and forth like they were on patrol. But they were much too small to stop me. I trailed my foot in the water. It looked deep. I pulled up a reed and dipped it in to test. It was deep. I stopped. Then I told myself: 'You won't die unless it's deep, stupid.'

I jumped down, like someone had pushed me, and then steadied myself among the weeds. Water seeped through my shoes. I squelched forwards, eddies swirling round my feet, until I was in the middle of the river with the current tugging me down. I thought about the world under water. I saw the mobile in my hand. I'd do all sorts of things with it. I'd get everything I wanted. I'd really spoil myself, the way no one had ever done before.

But something didn't make sense. How could heaven be down below? It should be up above. I didn't understand. But unless I figured it out, my plan wouldn't work.

I clambered out of the river and rushed off to ask the priest. His house was a mess, as if he'd given up on life. He told me that after someone died, they had to spend a bit of time in the underworld before they went up to heaven.

'You mean, under the water?' I said.

'Where the water is deepest, there's a secret tunnel which leads directly to heaven. Just like when you dig down into the earth, you reach America,' he explained.

Now I really didn't get it. It wasn't that I thought the priest was lying, I just couldn't see who would come and take me up.

'I want to go to heaven,' I said.

'To America?'

'To where my big sister is.' The priest burst out laughing. I carried on. 'If I die will you make sure I get to heaven?'

He stopped laughing and looked straight at me. 'No, I can't,' he said.

'Why not?'

'Because I'll die before you.'

'What if I die first?'

'Impossible.'

'But if I do?'

'That's not going to happen.'

Why didn't he understand? I was going to tell him I wanted to die, but then I realised he'd tell my dad.

'I'll definitely die before you,' he grumbled. An odd look came over his face. 'Hey, are you going to heaven to find your big sister?'

I nodded.

'And once you've found her, what will you do then?'

'I want her mobile…'

'And what if she doesn't give it to you?'

'I'll get it off her.' I said.

'You little swine!' he shouted. 'You don't love her, you just want to grab her phone off her. You're as heartless as all men in this world. What's so special about that phone?'

Suddenly I realised that the priest wanted the phone. That's why he wanted to die before me, it was all a trick. He was rushing off to heaven to snatch the phone from her before me.

I had to get there first. I told him I was going home. Heaven was in the opposite direction, but I walked part of the way home so he wouldn't know what I was up to. Then I turned off the road, went back down to the river and waded in. Then I stopped. Who was going to make sure I went up to heaven? I looked up at the cliffs. The highest stones went the deepest when they crashed into the water. If I jumped from the top, I'd go right down into the depths for sure, and that's where the priest said the passage was which led straight to heaven. I should be able to find it under the water. I ran to the top of the hill and scrambled up the cliff. It towered high over the village and fell sheer to the river. It was dangerous, but with only one step I could take off and fly.

The hills billowed away into the distance like waves, until they merged with the cloudy sky. A few birds flew past, and were gone. Had they disappeared into heaven up there? But then how did heaven join up with the underworld. It didn't make sense.

'Hey! Get down off there! It's dangerous!'

Someone was shouting at me.

'Can't you hear me? That's no place for kids. Come back here!'

The man wore a tatty old cloak woven out of rushes and carried a hoe. He was obviously dirt poor. I didn't want to go back to a life like his, I wanted to go to heaven. And besides, what was it to do with him? I was just about to jump when he grabbed me. He dragged me away from the edge and told me to go back to the village. But as soon as I was out of his sight I ran further along the cliff and headed back up.

Blockhead and Iron Egg were there. What were they up to? I ducked down and turned to go, but they chased after me calling out 'Come and play with us!'

I said I didn't want to.

'You're still angry about the puppies, aren't you' said Blockhead.

Puppies? I looked at him blankly. Then I remembered that Blockhead's big sandy dog had just given birth to a bunch of puppies. He hadn't let me stroke them. He said I'd make them choke because my hands smelled of death. But he let Iron Egg sneak into the house and stroke them.

'Don't get angry,' he said. 'I'll let you stroke them too.'

But his voice sounded fuzzy and his face was blurred, as if I was looking at him through a pane of glass. Those puppies seemed so long ago. And it was true, I really did smell of death. I was dead already. I didn't care about any of that old stuff. That's what happens when someone dies. You have nothing to do with anything any more.

'Don't worry about it,' I said.

'You're not angry?' asked Blockhead.

'No.'

'Then you'll play with us?

185

'No.'

'Then you must be still angry!' said Iron Egg.

'I'm not,' I said. 'I've got something to do.'

That told them. That was the kind of thing grown-ups said. Blockhead and Iron Egg had always been mean to me. If they didn't feel like playing, they didn't. And if they wanted to play with me, then of course I had to. But now I could tell them to get lost because I didn't need them any more.

'What?' they asked.

I didn't want to tell them. I couldn't.

'Tell us. Please, please!' they begged. Iron Egg looked really worried. He was jigging on the spot like he had to pee. He was pleading with me. This was great. I told them about the mobile phone.

'Where is it?' said Blockhead. 'We can all play with it.'

I smelled a rat. If they came along, there'd be three of us trying to grab the phone. And they'd always been better at grabbing than me.

'There's no phone. I was just kidding.' I said.

'There is. You're lying.'

'I'm not.'

'You are. You're still angry about the puppies!'

Why did they keep going on about the puppies? Those tiny puppies weren't going to stop me. I'd wasted too much time already. What if the priest worked out what I was up to and died before I did? And it was getting dark.

'I'm not,' I snapped.

'Look! Look, you're angry,' said Blockhead. 'I'll go and get one of the puppies for you to stroke. I'll bring it here.'

I really wasn't bothered, but he insisted: 'I'm going now. Wait here.'

Blockhead grabbed Iron Egg's arm, but Iron Egg said he'd stay and keep an eye on me. They were such a pain. Blockhead disappeared into the undergrowth and Iron Egg made a face at his retreating back. I couldn't believe it.

'But Blockhead let you stroke the puppies,' I said.

'Actually I didn't stroke them,' said Iron Egg. 'I only touched the very tip of the tip of the fur.' He held out his hand, his fingers reaching out into thin air. 'Blockhead's the meanest, meanest, meanest, meanest, meanest, meanest, meanest, meanest meanie,' he snarled.

I couldn't believe he was talking about Blockhead like that. It was brilliant.

'I've got something to show you,' said Iron Egg. 'A thirteen-colour toad.'

'A thirteen-colour toad?' I yelped.

'I found one. I hid it in a cave on North Hill.'

That was impossible. How could Iron Egg have got hold of something from a fairy tale? He must have made a mistake.

'Come this way,' said Iron Egg, and pulled my hand. I didn't care about the frog, I just wanted a friend. I forgot about dying. The only reason I wanted to die before was that I didn't have a best friend. We headed off towards North Hill. It was pretty tough going, but I tried to stroll along as if it was nothing. I started to puff and pant, larking around like I was exhausted. He roared with laughter.

I'd never noticed how thin he was before. The soles of his shoes were worn right through.

'Iron Egg, I'll take you with me to heaven.' He didn't understand. 'I'll let you play with the mobile.'

'Great!' His eyes lit up. 'But I'll show you the frog first.'

'Don't worry about the frog,' I said. 'We're running out

of time.'

I started pulling him. His hand was hot and sweaty and kept slipping out of my grasp. I promised myself that I'd let him play with the phone. I'd give him the best things to play with. I'd give him everything, even if I had nothing. He could even play with the phone first.

I took him to the top, stood him at the edge and pointed far away into the misty distance.

'Look,' I said.

'Where's the phone? There's nothing there,' said Iron Egg.

'If you fly over there, you'll find it,' I said. I didn't explain how we had to drop into the river and then go up again. He wouldn't get it.

'I can't fly, I'm scared,' he said.

'What are you scared of? Going to heaven?'

He looked at me and said it again: 'I can't fly...'

But Batman could fly. I'd seen him on TV at a funeral in the city.

'Do it like Batman,' I said.

He shook his head. He'd never seen Batman.

'You open your wings, and you fly,' I said.

It didn't look like he believed me. I was starting to worry. It was getting late. Blockhead was heading back to the cliff with the puppy and when he didn't find us there he'd start looking. And there was the priest. He might have set out for heaven already. And when my dad discovered I was gone, he would come looking too. Our village was so tiny you could piss from one end of it to the other. It wouldn't take anyone long to find us on North Hill. Then it would all be over. The sun was setting, blood red now. We were standing on a rock hanging right over the edge of the drop. It was getting dark. Iron Egg was really annoying, he was such a loser. People like him, people who hadn't seen the world just didn't get it. You put something right in front of them and they just let it go.

'Come on, let's fly together,' I said. But then I stopped. What if I took off and he decided not to? Better if I let him go first.

'Fly!' I said. 'Stand on tip-toe, like this. Shut your eyes.'

I shut mine.

'Jump!' I shouted.

I opened my eyes but he was still standing there, swaying on the edge. I gave him a push. He went down.

Way below, a bird soared into the air with a squawk.

I leaned over but I couldn't see him. He must have plunged into the depths of the river down below. Or maybe that bird was him, and he'd gone straight to heaven without needing to dive into the water. The priest had tricked me. Going straight to heaven was a much better idea than going there through the river. Just then I heard my mum calling me. Smoke curled from the chimneys of the village down below in the evening sunshine. She was calling me in for dinner. I could smell it. I was so hungry. Maybe I didn't have to go to heaven on my own. I could go with my mum. She wouldn't snatch the phone off me, she was always giving me things, even if she didn't have anything much herself. I'd be good to her and take her with me. I'd go down the mountain to get her even though I might bump into my dad or anyone, even if they all wanted to come too. I definitely had to get my mum. I ran home as quickly as I could.

Are you sure about this?

189

Chen Xiwo

You can shut the book now.
Do you choose to read on?

The Man with the Knife

The famous critic lies back on the sofa, a little pissed. They're back at the young poet's flat after she has taken him out for dinner – he said he'd help make her a star of the poetry world. It's difficult to be a star as a poet, he says. She'll have to work hard.

She asks him if he wants some tea. If he sobers up a bit they can carry on talking poetry. Rilke and Yeats, even Foucault and Modernism – an ongoing story according to Fredric Jameson. But there's only one now he can think about – he needs a slash.

She listens to the flow in the bathroom. She feels nothing – it just sounds like a running tap. Her three year old sounds just the same when he does a pee. Sometimes he misses the toilet and it goes on the floor. Will this man do the same? She likes things to be clean, but he is a guest, after all.

He comes back in without doing up his belt. He sits down across from her and she sees he hasn't done up his zip either. She switches to the other sofa, so she's sideways on.

What about an orange? That might sober him up. She peels one, but he doesn't take it. She puts it into his unresisting hand and then tries to pop a segment in his mouth, but finds she has lost her balance and falls on top of him. Some of the orange squashes in her hand and the rest flies across the room. His trousers are coming off.

She jumps up to get the fruit. She says nothing. What can she say to this famous poet? She was calling him teacher a minute ago. Maybe it was an accident. Maybe he's just drunk.

He's not drunk. He knows just what he's doing, and is delighted that she's resisting. It's boring when they give in straight away. He's a famous poet, so they almost all give in. But he likes a bit of resistance first, however feeble, a bit of naughtiness and giggling. Or a few cries of 'No! Don't do that!' which actually mean 'Yes.' Sometimes, of course, they are too keen. Like that girl in Suzhou with a condom all ready. That really put him off.

This woman is trying to get away from him. That turns him on. She's crouching on the floor with her back to him. He grabs her from behind.

Now it's perfectly clear what he's up to, what kind of man he is. But she isn't that kind of woman. She just wants to write poems. Of course she wants to be famous too, and successful. What can she do? She doesn't want to offend him, so she keeps still at first – if she moves he'll know she's trying to stop him. Then she hauls herself up and drags him to the sofa. But when she lets go, he grabs her and pulls her down with him. She's lying on top of him, with his arms around her.

She struggles out of his embrace, but he keeps holding on to her wrist. She tries to pull away, smoothing her mussed-up hair.

'I'll go and get you some tea,' she says.

He shakes his head.

'I don't want tea. I want you.'

She gives him a stupid smile, the kind of smile she makes if a man starts telling dirty jokes at a work dinner, as if she doesn't understand.

'Come on!' he says.

She shakes her head. But she still doesn't want to offend him. She rubs her neck, giggles and simpers 'I don't want to.'

'Yes you do.'

'I don't.'

'You do!' He starts jerking her arm back and forth. This is horribly embarrassing. Then he gives a hard, insistent tug, so she lands on top of him. He flips over on top of her and stares down. She can't look away. It's awful. She just has to keep smiling.

There's something sharp, like a knife, prodding her soft flesh. Where on earth has he got a knife from?

She has to get away from the knife, but he's right on top of her. She looks around wildly, her eyes falling on a photograph of her husband on the low table.

'I'm married … ' she says.

'He's not here, is he?' He definitely isn't drunk. He reaches out and puts the picture face down on the table. 'Gone.'

It's true. There's no one else in the flat apart from her son, asleep in his bedroom. The housekeeper went home when she brought the professor back. What did the woman think? … But why does that matter? If no one finds out, would that make it OK? She doesn't know. The worst thing is he's not drunk. She can't use that as an excuse.

He's trying to pull down her trousers. She holds on to them tight. The more she resists, the harder he pulls. Pulling the trousers off a respectable woman like this one creates so much more tension than with a girl who's always ready to drop them. Tension is something he particularly likes to focus on when he's reviewing poetry. The magic of poetry is all about tension.

The lamp beside the sofa falls with a crash. A wail from the child's bedroom. He freezes for a second and she breaks free. The boy comes out of his bedroom and she gathers him into her arms.

Seeing the child is a bit of a turn-off.

'Say hello to Uncle,' she says to the boy, thinking he can buy her some time.

'Hello, Uncle,' says the boy.

The professor gives a half-hearted grunt. The child pulls free of his mother's embrace and begins to play.

'Get him back to bed,' he tells her.

'Let him play a bit.'

He turns to the child.

'Go back to bed, little boy.' Trying to be patient.

'No.'

He'll just have to wait.

Time passes slowly.

'Go on, be a good boy,' he tries again. 'Go back to bed.'

'Don't want to.'

Furious, he grabs the child and heads for the bedroom. The child struggles. He puts him down inside. The child runs out again. What a pest! He carries him back in and plonks him down on the floor. The child starts wailing. She rushes in.

'What do you think you're doing?' she shrieks. She certainly isn't calling him teacher any more.

She picks up the child and tucks him into his cot. Why is the professor being such a pain? She doesn't dare get rid of him. She wants something from him. She's using him, and he wants to use her too, of course. He's a man, and wants what men want. You're a woman, she says to herself, you're only doing what women do to get what they want. Nothing wrong with that.

The child falls asleep. Back in the living room the professor leers at her.

He pounces on her again.

'You really want this?' she asks.

'Yes.'

'You're not worried I'll tell?'

'Say what you want.'

He leads her into the bedroom and pushes her down on to the bed. He peels off her trousers. She doesn't really struggle.

She wonders what underwear she has on. Oh good, the lacy ones.

By the time they're off, she isn't struggling any more.

He starts scrabbling with his own clothes, so she jumps up to get a condom. She absolutely mustn't get pregnant. There's a spare in the drawer from the last time her husband was home. She lies back on the bed, waiting, the condom in her hand.

Is she up for it now? He's disappointed, just like with the girl in Suzhou. What the hell, he's going to screw her anyway.

She shuts her eyes and waits for it to be over. But there's nothing pushing inside. She can't even feel that knife-sharp erection. What's he doing? She opens her eyes. The condom is still in his hand. The other hand is pumping up and down, but his penis is soft. She sits up. It's not her fault he's not hard any more. But he pushes her back down with the same hand that has been working on his penis. Horrible.

'You can't get it up . . .' she mutters.

'Who says?' he shouts. This has never happened before. Maybe he got too excited at the thought of tearing into her – and she's just given in. There he is, about to rip her modesty away, and it turns out she has none. He's totally empty. He beats at his cock, hard, but it's no good. This is going nowhere. He kisses her cheeks, her neck, her breasts. He rubs himself against her, turning her over and back again.

She's getting tired of all this. Finally he stops. He must be ready. All she has to do is open her legs for that knife. She turns over to face him, the folds of skin on her belly flopping like the neck of a Sharpei dog. He goes soft again. The only way she can get this over with is to sharpen his knife for him. She props herself up.

'Lie down,' she says.

He's surprised, but does as she says. She grabs hold of his penis. After all, her husband has one. All men do. Once a man is just a penis, everything is simple.

Now he's the one who's embarrassed, who tries to twist away.

'Keep still,' she orders.

She lays him out flat, his skin white as boiled pork. She's the butcher.

Her hand is cold as ice, but somehow he feels a shiver of pleasure. Ice-cold pleasure. It's as if he's observing himself from a great distance. He can really feel the chills of pleasure and see himself enjoying it. But what about her? She's not enjoying it at all, just getting a result. That's no good at all.

'You like it?' he asks.

She's taken aback. 'Of course.'

'Liar.'

'No.' She's disgusted. He wants her to enjoy it as well?

'It's ... really ... nice.' She doesn't sound convincing. They're both faking it. Just going through the motions.

'Liar.'

'Oh, shut up!' she shouts. The thing in her hand is responding less and less. She pumps it up and down, but it's like pulling on an elephant's trunk, his foreskin stretching and shrinking back. It's starting to hurt. He yelps.

She bends over him and takes it in her mouth. Pretend it's chewing pork, she thinks.

He is appalled.

Normally he loves putting his dirtiest part into the cleanest part of a woman. He lifts the woman's hair, so he can watch her mouth going at him. But this isn't working at all.

He has to let her do it, she thinks, otherwise he'll never get hard. She shoves him back down. At last his penis fills her mouth. She sits back and it stands up as stiff as a snake. It feels strange, as if it's no longer part of his body.

Now they can get it over with. But he doesn't move. What is she going to do if he goes soft again? She skips the condom, gets on top and pushes him in. There's something not quite right, so she shifts slightly. That's better. She can't believe it feels right with a man who is not her husband. Well, you can get used to anything.

He's not happy.

'Don't move,' she says. 'It'll be good in a minute!'

'No . . .'

Isn't this what he's after? Maybe he wants to mess around a bit more, so he won't come too soon. Well tough! She'll make him come now. A man behaves himself once he's shot his load.

'Give it to me,' she says.

'Really?'

'Really!' She speeds up. Just let him come.

'Then let me hear you.'

Was he crazy?

'Go on, make some noise,' he says. 'You want it, and it's good, so let me hear you shout.'

She cries out.

'Louder!'

She does it again.

'Rubbish,' he says and tries to throw her off.

She's just faking it. She doesn't feel like shouting, the noise just comes mechanically from her vocal chords and out of her mouth. She's a whore. But isn't he a whore too, a literary whore? He's sold his soul already. Only the flesh remains. When did that happen?

The first time he had sex with a girl she didn't make a noise, she bit him hard on the shoulder. That was his wife. He was dirt poor back then, living on steamed buns, so he could devote himself to his writing. He spent hours revising his work, polishing it, then timidly paid court to editors and begged them to publish it. But his idealism is long gone, along with his fine feelings. He is at one remove from everything, from this. He wants out.

But how much longer will this drag on for if he gets up now? She's frantic.

'I'm telling the truth!' she insists.

'All right, I'll tell the truth too. You really want to know what I think of your poems?'

She nods.

'They're very poor. In fact they're terrible.'

She never believed he really liked her poetry, but his words are a slap in the face.

'You're totally without talent.'

It's like someone has pushed her under the waves and held her down. She wants to get away, but what then? He's inside her already. Damn him! How dare he talk about poetry at a time like this? Some poet! But he really is a poet, of course, and the most important poet on the whole scene.

Suddenly she is free, turned on by his blunt speaking.

'All right then, say what you want.'

She starts moving on top of him again. He'll have to help with her career, now she's let him do it to her. Harder, faster, she rocks with abandon. She's actually enjoying it.

He's the one who's worried now. She's flipped it all around, she's turned his own weapon on him. She's jerking up and down like a suction pump. He's not enjoying it, not at all. But she can still make him ejaculate. There's nothing he can do about it. Like water spurting out of a pipe.

He comes.

She jumps off and runs to the bathroom. A trickle of semen oozes on to his belly.

What am I doing here? he wonders. The room is empty and still. The semen is cold, like a runny nose on a winter's day.

When she comes back, she's fully dressed. She smiles. He shivers and a few more drops of semen leak out.

'Go on, be as rude as you like,' she says.

What does she mean?

'I wasn't being rude … '

'Write me a poetry review – a real hatchet job.'

'I'm going home … '

'So you've had your fun and now you want to pull up your trousers and go.'

'I didn't have any fun,' he mutters weakly. It's not very convincing.

'OK,' she sighs. 'I'll do it again, so you can enjoy it.'

He watches, appalled, as she begins to strip.

'No!' he shouts.

She flashes a smile and carries on unwrapping her flabby body. A great big sow. The worst thing is, he's getting hard again. His penis rears up greedily. He frantically tries to pull his trousers over it but it pokes up anyway. A law unto itself. He's only a man after all, and all men are like that, all carrying those ugly things around with them. It's what makes a man strong. But his strength is a weakness now.

She comes closer. What can he do? He shrinks back.

But she's not asking for anything difficult. He does it all the time. Flattering here, stabbing someone in the back over there, wherever it gains him an advantage.

'Your pen's your knife, isn't it?' she says. 'That's what your job's about. And you've certainly got a sharp knife.'

A knife! He leaps up and makes a dive for the kitchen. There'll be a knife in there.

She follows him in confusion, sees him grab a knife.

'Don't kill me!' she shouts. 'It's all right, you don't have to write anything about me. Whatever you want, I'll do it, whatever it is … '

He brandishes the knife.

She shrieks. A wail of terror from the child. She runs to the boy's bedroom. Is he coming after her? She holds the child in her arms and looks through the door.

The man is standing there, the knife dangling at his crotch. It is covered in blood. There's something wrong with his body. Something is missing.

The Man with the Knife

It hangs from the knife.

You have corrupted my imagination and inflamed my blood. I am beginning to enjoy all this.

'It is true that the act of writing is dancing with shackles on, but these should be artistic shackles, not political ones.'
Chen Xiwo

www.fortysix.tv